Maison Angelique

ROWENA WYLDE
&
EMILY HUSSEY

A division of Winsome Enterprises Pty Ltd
Adelaide, South Australia

Contents

1 - Thursday 1

2 – Start of the Week 24

3 – The Soiree 45

4 – Wednesday and a Black Volvo 55

5 – A Breach in Security 69

6 – Making Sense of it All 88

7 – Exploring Options 111

8 – Guess Who? 125

9 – An End to Executive Coaching 141

10 – A Job Offer 160

11 – Life in a Casino 178

12 – A Misunderstanding 195

13 – New Business Option 212

14 – The Launch of Maison Angelique 225

15 – A Cruise with a Difference 237

Before you go 257

Emily Hussey 258

Ambition and Passion 260

Also by Emily Hussey

Tales from Harrow
Wild Spirit
Wild Destiny
Wild Tempest
Wild Fire

Red Centre Series
Journey to the Heart
The Red Heart
Trust Your Heart
Follow Your Heart

Stand-alone Stories
Ambition and Passion
Maison Angelique

Sandy Bay Series
Secrets in Sandy Bay
Escape to Sandy Bay
Return to Sandy Bay

Collection of Short Stories
Romance in the Stone

1 - Thursday

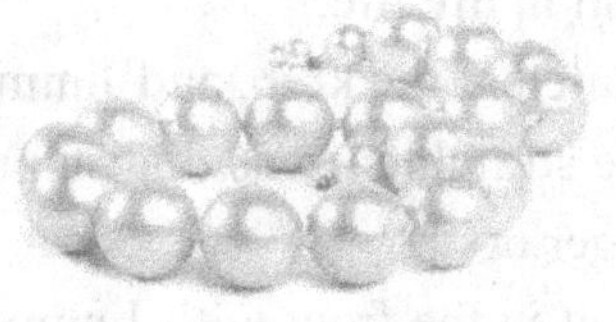

Anticipation made her toes curl and her heart dance a
rhythm of its own making. Choosing her outfit for the day
had seemed laughable, given the circumstances. She dressed
with extra care, smiling inwardly at herself. It wasn't as if the
clothes she wore would make any difference. Except for
Mattie and Jimmy, they wouldn't be seen. The difference lay
in how the clothes made her feel; powerful, desirable and in
control.

She wore her favourite Ted Baker dress, a navy midi,
slim fitting and with short fluted sleeves. She had fixed
sapphire and diamond studs to her ears and clipped the Tag
Heuer watch around her wrist. The Christian Louboutin
pumps matched the colour of the dress perfectly. After
surveying her reflection in the mirror, she had slipped her
arms into her coat, another Ted Baker favourite, and then she
was ready.

A ping on her phone told her that Jimmy waited outside. "Mattie! Grab your bag, it's time to go."

A small whirlwind clattered down the stairs and picked up the backpack, waiting by the door. "You smell nice, Mum."

"Thank you. It's nice to know I'm appreciated by the number one man in my life."

The car waited at the kerb, and Jimmy leaned against the front fender. He straightened as they approached and opened the rear passenger door.

"I want to sit in the front with Jimmy."

The driver glanced at her. She shrugged. Up to you. He opened the front passenger door as well.

"Okay. You can tell me the way."

Mattie giggled at the familiar joke. "Same as yesterday, and same as the day before that."

"Good. We won't get lost then."

Five minutes later, they drew up at the school gates. Mattie climbed out of the car and slung his pack over his shoulder. Angela slid out of the back seat and moved to give her son a hug, but he stepped back with a wave.

"See ya tonight."

He dashed through the gate, heading for a couple of other boys his own age.

"Jimmy, did you see that? He didn't want to give me a hug!"

"He's growing up, Miss Angelique. That's what boys do."

"I know, but…" She climbed back into the car and fastened her seatbelt. Letting go was harder than she had expected. Jimmy had thoughtfully provided her with the paper to read in the car, but the words blurred before her eyes. How could she focus on mundane news, knowing what day it was?

"You don't mind if I make myself comfortable, do you? It feels a little hot in here."

Angelique began a slow strip, her eyes fixed on the man standing by the window. Every action was calculated to tease the man watching her. He sipped his champagne, his eyes raking her body as each item of clothing was removed. She relished the lingering gaze. In her mind, his fingers were touching her, his lips and then his tongue. She had anticipated this moment, through Monday, Tuesday and then Wednesday.

Dressed only in bra and panties, delicate scraps of lilac silk and lace, Angelique moved to join him; her eyes all the while fixed on his. The anticipation sent a wave of sweet heat, starting from her centre of pleasure and sweeping outwards.

"It's nothing to the heat I'm feeling. You're the most enticing of women," he murmured into her hair. "I know I've said it before, but if I could bottle you, I'd make a fortune."

Kneeling before him, she removed his shoes, first one and then the other. Rising, she reached for his belt, and unbuckled it with practiced hands before moving to the buttons on his shirt. Breaking eye contact, Angelique kissed his bare chest, running her fingers over the muscled physique.

With a muted growl of desire, he was galvanised into action, stripping off the rest of his clothes and leaving her in no doubt at the level of his desire. Now it was his turn. Drawing her to the bed, he unclipped her bra and slid off her underwear.

She let her fingers do the talking, caressing his body, teasing and tantalising. She slid against the length of him and the pressure of his chest against hers caused her nipples to harden, signalling her own desire. In a well-practised action, she reached for the condom waiting on the bedside table and slid it over his burgeoning cock. They strained against each other, their bodies telegraphing the passion ignited by memories of past unions. Their appetites for each other were insatiable, but each treasured the moment, prolonging sensation until resistance was impossible. Their coupling was fierce and gluttonous, with both of them generous yet demanding of the other.

Sated, they lay side by side, his hand resting possessively on her thigh. Angelique closed her eyes, focussing on the pressure of each digit on her bare skin. *Higher–it's not far, c'mon, just a little higher.*

Instead, he rolled towards her and cupped a breast, teasing a nipple between thumb and forefinger. "This doesn't have to end here, surely? We could catch up this evening— meet for dinner even. His voice was still husky with desire.

If only she could be certain he wanted her for herself and not what she did for him.

Don't go there. Don't even think about it.

4

"You know that's not possible. We see each other on Thursday. That's the agreement." She struggled to maintain a neutral tone. He could never know how much of an effort it was to enforce the limitations of their contact. She wished it was different. Perhaps one day…

"Surely variations to the agreement are possible? I know some very good lawyers if that's any help." He moved his attention to the other breast.

She swatted his hand away. "Idiot! How exactly would you brief your corporate lawyer?" She assumed a formal tone. "I spend time each Thursday with a woman engaged in mind-blowing sexual congress and wish to extend the time allocated for the liaison. Please draft a variation to our unwritten contract."

His theatrical sigh filled the room. "Since you put it like that, it might raise a few questions. Just warning you though, I won't give up trying."

"I'd be surprised if you did." *Disappointed even, but I won't let on to that fact.* The idea that he wanted to spend more time in her company was comforting. In her mind, she envisioned a future in which they spent every day together, and not just in bed. It was an impossible dream. Better not to think about it.

"What drives a woman like you?" he asked, propping himself up on an elbow so he could look at her. "Surely you have a life outside this apartment?"

"A woman like me? What you're really asking is how I came to provide the services I do?"

"Well, sort of… I know you mix in salubrious circles because of where I met you but beyond that you're an enigma. What are your passions? What drives you?"

Angela looked at him a moment. His questions were straying into her no-go zone. "Well ballet was always a passion. I trained with the Australian Ballet School, but I grew too tall and my toes never coped well with on point work, so I gave it up."

She opened her eyes wide, willing him to imagine her pirouetting across a stage. "I thought I might put my long legs to good use so I took up cycling. I set my sights on the Olympics, but riding round and round the velodrome made me dizzy so I gave that up too."

"You? An Olympic cyclist? The ballet dancer I was prepared to believe but somehow I never pictured you in competitive sport."

"No? Well how do you picture me?"

He furrowed his brow as he pondered the question. "As to how I picture you… I think probably the CEO of a corporation. Something that sees you nominated for businesswoman of the year."

"Now you've surprised me. What made you say that?" Of all the things he might have said, this was the most unexpected.

"You've always given me the impression of knowing what you want and being driven. I just didn't know by what. You hold your own in a conversation, and on one of my previous visits, I noticed a book on share analysis on top of your drink's cabinet. It was bookmarked partway through, so I assume you'd been reading it. That tells me you have an interest in the financial markets. Don't quote me, but all those little things added up to a businesswoman of note."

He trailed a finger down a path between her breasts and circling around her belly, following the path with his eyes before looking back at hers. His mouth twitched with barely suppressed humour. "I think I like my version better than either a ballet dancer or a cyclist."

Damn. I didn't fool him one bit. Actually, I like his version better too.

Knowing he would have to leave soon, Angelique slid off the bed and put on her robe, fastening the belt around her waist. "More champagne?" she asked.

"I'll keep you company, but only half a glass. I need a clear head for the rest of the day."

She took the bottle from the cooler and filled both their glasses before passing his over and settling herself back against the bed head. She enjoyed the camaraderie of this time just as much as what went before. Sometimes he would talk about his business; other times his travels or perhaps his dreams for the future. It was idle conversation, but she soaked it all up.

He glanced at the bedside clock, and groaned. "Look at the time. I've got to go. I could happily stay here all day."

He leaned over and pulling her robe aside, kissed the soft peak of the closest breast before disappearing into the ensuite. Angelique heard the shower running moments after he shut the door.

She selected a new music track and placed the empty bottle in the kitchen. When he emerged from the bathroom, he smelt of the lavender and the sandalwood body wash she kept there. On him, the scent was manly. For a few moments, she took comfort in the resemblance of domesticity. If only.

She had boiled the jug and had a cup of tea waiting, just as he liked it. He always had a quick cup of tea as he dressed.

He sipped appreciatively, a look of bliss on his face. "You know I only come here for the cup of tea. I don't know what your blend is but it's the best cup of tea I get all week."

"It's not the tea," she responded with an alluring pout, "but the person who brews it that makes the difference."

"I can believe it," he responded. "I've felt your magic touch."

He drained the cup and placed it on the table beside the envelope. "Next week?"

She walked him to the door where he turned and kissed her gently, one hand possessively on her butt and the other drawing her close. She already felt bereft.

"Next week," she agreed. It would soon be the weekend, and those days would be filled with home life, but Monday to Wednesday would go slowly.

Closing the door behind him, she crossed to the table and picked up the envelope, depositing it into the safe in the next room. There was no need to check the contents. It would be correct.

It was her turn for a shower, washing away all trace of their union before changing into her home clothes. Scooping up the towels and bedsheets, she dropped them into the laundry basket. The cleaner would take care of those. She needed to hurry. Jimmy would be waiting downstairs.

She made a quick call. "Mr Thursday has left the building. Be down soon, Jimmy."

There was no need to shut the curtains. No-one else could see in at this level. She glanced out of the window by the dining table. Afternoon shadows were already stretching across the bay. A passenger ferry cruised past, and she could see the interior lights were on. The previously bright blues and golden highlights now morphed into silvers and muted shades. It was time to get her skates on. With one last check that everything was in order, she locked the safe and let herself out of the apartment, securing the door behind her. She slid into the back seat of the Mercedes saloon, grateful as ever for the anonymity of the dark tinted windows.

"Everything under control Miss Angelique?"

"As always, Jimmy. Take me home."

As Angela walked up the path to the town house the front door opened and a small individual flew out the door. This was the person who made it all worthwhile.

"Mum! I got to be class captain today!"

"Mattie, that's wonderful. I'm so pleased for you sweetheart. Where's your nan?"

"She's in the kitchen. I think she's making a cup of tea."

Angela followed her son down the passage to the kitchen where indeed her mother was sitting with a cup of tea and a magazine.

"Hello dear," the older woman said, lifting her face for a kiss. "How was work today?"

Angela fetched a cup and saucer from the cupboard and poured herself some tea from the pot. No tea bags for her mother.

"Oh, you know… more of the same. Nothing particularly special."

"Jimmy's keeping well?" her mother asked.

"He never misses a beat. He has a cast-iron constitution."

"Still, you're so lucky to have that job; good security and Jimmy thrown in as well. I've said it before— doing that bookkeeping course was the smartest thing you ever did. Without that, you'd never have got the job with Sasha Berkowitz and then where would you be?"

It was her mother's frequent refrain. The bookkeeping course had been useful and it *had* got her the job with Sasha, but it didn't end up being quite the role her mother thought. She wouldn't find out either. Angelique's business cards said 'Executive Coaching', but her mother had no idea about the sensual services that were classified as *executive coaching*, and hadn't seen those cards either. Angela made sure of that.

"Did I mention I've invested in a few shares, Mum? I thought it was time I made some provision for the future."

Louise Benson looked most surprised. "I didn't think you knew much about the stock market. I hope you're not taking any risks."

Angela tried not to smile. Her mother's response was predictable. Louise had raised Angela on her own, and was conscious of the financial pressures of being a sole parent.

"Sasha's husband Renato has been teaching me about investment strategies. I'm not doing anything rash, Mum, but I need to consolidate the future for Matthew and myself. Besides, how will I look after you if I don't have some investments behind me?"

"I've managed up until now and I'm sure I'll continue to do so. Anyway, seeing as you're home, I'll get going myself." She rose from her chair and picked up her bag. "I've put a casserole in the oven. It's almost ready to come out. Don't forget it. See you tomorrow, love."

Angela waved her mother off, grateful as ever she had someone reliable to care for Matthew after school. Working would have been more difficult without that arrangement in place. Particularly with the sort of work she did. Besides which, Matthew was part of her private life. Nobody else was going to intrude on that.

Jimmy was waiting by the time she got back from walking Matthew to school the next morning. The black saloon was parked out the front of her townhouse, and Jimmy was reading the morning paper. He was reliable and discreet, and always a useful source of information. She kept him waiting a few more minutes while she grabbed her bag from inside and locked up. As customary, she slid into the back seat, and he handed her a cup of coffee, just as she liked it. She loved the way he looked after her.

"Good morning Miss Angelique. Where to today?"

"Can we detour past the beauty salon on Gibson Street? My nails need a touch up. After that it's straight to the apartment. I have some work to do before Mr Friday arrives."

"Yes Ma'am. I see he was featured in the business section of the morning's paper. I left a copy on the seat in case you want to read up on the news before your meeting."

"Thank you. Most thoughtful of you, Jimmy."

His eyes met hers with a smile in the rear vision mirror. He had come with Sasha's recommendation and was worth every cent she paid him. Her mother believed Jimmy was employed by Sasha, and Angela didn't correct her. It wasn't lying, she told herself – well okay it was, but only by omission. She trusted him implicitly. He was more than a driver; his background in security meant he had her safety at heart as well. Her mother also thought it was cute that Jimmy referred to her daughter as 'Miss Angelique'. Angela remained sphinx-like on that issue as well.

Flipping through the paper she found the article to which he referred. Mr Friday was involved in high level negotiations for a new casino and resort development in an Asian country and the article dealt with political and cultural obstacles. Scanning the rest of the paper, her attention was drawn by a reference to Johnson Hydrology and their activities in the Middle East. She made a mental note to review the information in greater detail. It paid to keep on top of the business dealings of her clients.

"Looks like a beautiful weekend coming up." Jimmy interrupted her thoughts.

"I think you're right. I might take Matthew to the beach. It's time we both got some fresh air in our lungs."

There was a free parking space close to the salon, which was unusual given the inner-city location. The street of terraced buildings had undergone many reinventions over the last century and was now experiencing a surge of gentrification. Neighbouring premises accommodated trendy cafés, complete with footpath tables and water bowls for the dogs, or boutiques selling quirky designer clothes. The street hadn't yet made a name for itself as a 'destination' but was getting there.

Jimmy expertly reversed into the car space. Angela almost expected him to do it with only one hand on the wheel. "I won't be long. Can I get you another coffee?"

"I've had two already this morning, so I'll pass on that. I've got a book with me and I can listen to the radio. Take your time; I'll be fine."

Jimmy would make some woman the perfect husband. She'd never heard him mention a partner though and knew better than to ask.

The door to the salon buzzed as she pushed it open, and Gracie, the proprietor came to greet her. They settled themselves at a workstation, and Angela proffered her hands.

"Tell me what's been happening lately in your world," Gracie said as she bent over Angela's nails.

"Just the usual. Mattie's growing taller and is learning to answer back. Studies are progressing well." She eyed Gracie's belly. "How about you? You can't have long to go now."

Gracie straightened up with a protective hand on the bulge. "I can't complain really, but I had thought the second baby would be easier than this. I get so tired!"

"Hardly surprising. You're running around after a toddler and working in your business as well as being in an advanced stage of pregnancy. Can't you cut back on your hours?"

Gracie resumed her work, her tongue protruding slightly as the focused on delivering lacquer with the required steady strokes. She paused, reviewing her work under a lamp before answering. "I would love to cut back, but with a new baby on the way, finances are stretched. I'm delaying the appointment of a replacement technician as long as I can. I'd really like more time to spend with my family though."

"That's a perfectly reasonable desire but I understand the money issues," Angela said. "I hope you find a solution soon. Don't forget to let me know when the baby arrives. I can't wait to meet him or her."

"Sure. I'll make a note of it."

That's not an enthusiastic response. She really must be tired. If Jimmy wasn't waiting outside, she might have discussed the matter further, but it wasn't really her business.

When she paid up ten minutes later, Angela impulsively gave Gracie a hug. "Put your feet up for a while, at least. I'll keep in touch." The smile she got in response was wan rather than warm.

When she hurried outside to the car, Jimmy was still seated behind the wheel, head tilted back and a soft snore emanating from his partially open mouth. He jerked awake as she opened the car door, turning towards her with an innocent expression.

"Just resting my eyes, Miss Angelique."

Sure, Jimmy. "Shall we go?"

They pulled into the underground car park and passed through the security grill that provided additional privacy. Jimmy always insisted she wait until the grill shut behind them before she exited the car. "Can't be too careful," he usually said. Angelique thought it a little extreme but was happy to oblige him.

Jimmy was of indiscriminate age, and had the stocky, compact build of one who could look after himself. His wardrobe consisted entirely of black. He didn't need to stand out. As he once told her, it was better if he didn't. He didn't disclose much about his background either, but they all had their secrets.

Angela slid out of the back seat, throwing a farewell over her shoulder as she did. "Same time as usual Jimmy. See you this afternoon."

With her security access, the elevator took her directly to the penthouse apartment. She paused on entry, taking in the view. Jimmy was right. There was some beautiful weather coming up. The picture windows overlooked the bay, and she never tired of watching the boats and the water activity. Today, it was glorious.

She wished she had artistic talents. Then she could capture the myriad of colours in paint—the blue-greens on the water and the dancing patterns of sunlight. An endless parade of boats passed by, with the wake spreading out to gently nudge the vessels moored at the water's edge.

Even on cloudy days, the scenery could be spectacular. It was one of the things that had drawn her to this apartment – that and the security features. Sasha had helped finance it but with her repayment schedule, she would soon have it paid off.

The second bedroom was set up as her office, and dropping her bag on a chair, she fired up the laptop. While it was running through its start-up routine, she checked the contents of the fridge. Champagne, strawberries, olives, cheese, milk – hmm, some shopping required to top up supplies.

She brought her lunch with her each day. While making lunch for Matthew to take to school, it was easy to make some for herself, and she didn't want to create too much domestic mess in the apartment. She passed up on the plastic lunch box for lacquered bento box, holding a variety of salads. She slid it into the fridge, sneaking a quick strawberry at the same time. It was juicier than she expected and she quickly wiped a dribble from the corner of her mouth with the back of her hand. Lucky she hadn't put lipstick on yet.

Completing the next module of her trading course took up most of the morning. She wasn't lying to her mother. Renato had taught her a lot about shares and investment in general, but she wanted more detailed knowledge and had enrolled in a course offered by the Stock Exchange. She needed to look to her future. She had built up a respectable portfolio but acquiring the knowledge to manage it effectively was important. If ever she couldn't sleep at night, it was for worrying about financial security for herself and her son.

She glanced at her watch. It was already lunchtime, although tummy rumbles had indicated that for a while. Not long before Mr Friday's appointment. She ate her sandwiches and tidied up. Time for Angelique. Stripping off the outer layer of 'mum clothes' revealed the expensive lingerie she wore beneath. Consulting her wardrobe and thinking of Mr Friday's tastes, she selected a black leather skirt, teamed with a leopard pattern top. She styled her hair into a tousled mane, slipped on her stilettos, and applied a slash of red lipstick. With a dab of sensuous perfume, she was ready. All that was left was to ensure the bedroom was in order and essential supplies were in easy reach.

On cue, the security buzzer sounded. She checked the monitor first, then pressed the button giving him access to the building. The elevator opened to the foyer, but she didn't open the door to the apartment before observing the monitor for the CCTV. This was another of Jimmy's requirements. *Can't be too careful.* Only when satisfied on the identity of the man outside the apartment did she open the door.

"Rrr ..." His reaction when he saw her was predictable. "Angelique, you really know how to bring out the animal in a man. I so need to see you today. This has been one helluva week."

"So it seems, if the papers are anything to go by. Come in, Tiger. Time to relax. Take your shoes off; loosen your tie while I fix you a drink. Scotch and soda, no ice?"

She knew that for all his bluff and bluster, it would take Mr Friday a while to unwind. It always did.

He was heir to a media chain. He was brought up with a sense of entitlement, and always knew the crown would be his. Despite that, he remained a nice man. The reins were still tightly held by his father and he was the 2IC, tested on some intense negotiations. His mother was heavily involved in philanthropic activities and insisted on his participation. He was not allowed to forget that his was a privileged position, not to be taken for granted.

"Shall I give you a massage? You look like you need it."

"Angelique, you have no idea how wonderful that would be."

"Surely you could engage a whole team of masseurs, one for every day of the week."

"I probably could, but none of them would quite have your magic touch. Plus, when I come here, I can put aside the business and everything that's happening. You're the one person I always feel doesn't care a fig for who I am or what I do. None of that matters when I walk through your door."

If he wasn't who he was, he would never get to walk through that door in the first place, but Angelique wasn't about to tell him that. Each of her clients was well-researched and qualified, as was their financial capacity.

"Come and lie down. I'll start with your back. Those shoulders will be tied up in knots."

She helped him out of his clothes and led him to the bed. After slipping her own outer clothes off as well, revealing matching leopard skin lingerie, she began working on the taut muscles, all the while imagining it was Mr Thursday who lay pliant beneath her fingers.

Never before had a client affected her like that man, but if she was to survive in her job, she had to remain impartial. She needed to focus on her client of the moment. That way she remained in control, and control was important. She worked her way down the torso in front of her, kneading first one buttock and then the other.

By the time she instructed Mr Friday to roll over, his erection strained upwards, and he moaned softly. With practiced hands, she massaged his chest, his stomach and then each leg and inner thigh, all the time ignoring the focus of his attention. Finally, when he could stand it no longer, he seized her and pulled her down onto the bed beside him.

"I'm going to explode in a minute. It's what the massage parlours call a happy ending. Come here, woman."

She managed to quickly sheath him before her remaining clothes were rapidly dispensed with and he leapt upon her. He was vocal in his release, joyful even. It was as though all the stress of the week was released in one swoop.

"Thank God it's Friday," he muttered, flopping onto his back. He lay there, spread-eagled and spent, his cock deflated. Not for long. With renewed enthusiasm, he was soon ready for a repeat performance, but this time requested they move in front of the windows. With Angelique on her knees, he entered her from behind, giving him a view of both her body beneath him and the fabulous vista below.

"This is absolutely a sight for sore eyes, on all counts." He leaned forward, cupping her swinging breasts. "I wish I could do this more often."

Angelique laughed. "Do you really think you could handle this more than one day a week? Anyway, you seem to travel a lot. You'd never have the time."

"You're right about that. I forget frequently where my home is. The business keeps me on the run, and the old man's expectations are high. He never slacks off, so I shouldn't either."

Mr Friday eased himself back into a sitting position, leaning against the side of the bed. He was silent for a moment, scratching idly at the beginnings of stubble on his chin.

She could almost hear the cogs whirring. She waited. He would come out with whatever was on his mind soon enough.

He stopped scratching and turned to look at her. "Do you ever get away—have a proper break, I mean?"

"Occasionally. Why?"

"I have an apartment in Sydney that I don't use often. It overlooks the Harbour and the Opera House. You could—"

No I couldn't. The offer would be an unnecessary complication.

"You lovely man, that's a fabulous suggestion. Maybe I can take you up on it one day but not at the moment." She reached out and laid a conciliatory hand on his arm. "Friday is your day, you know that."

"I know, I know… you've told me before. You're the only one who gets away with telling me what to do, or more to the point, what I can't do."

She smiled politely. Time for a diversion. Jumping up, she reached for the bowl of strawberries on the bedside table and popped one into his mouth before taking one for herself. The burst of sweetness must have worked its magic, because he didn't bring the subject up again for the remainder of his visit. She had never asked questions about his personal life, but had the impression that sometimes he was a little lonely. That was sad, but companionship went beyond her role.

When he left, Angelique completed her usual routine, showering and changing, The leather skirt went back into the cupboard, and the mum clothes re-appeared. She looked forward to the weekend and the time with her son. She reviewed the contents of the safe, extracting the funds she required for the coming week and putting payment for Jimmy to one side. Calling downstairs first, she locked up the apartment. It was time to go home.

The weekend passed in a flurry of domestic and kid-related activities. Saturday morning involved sport and, as promised, Angela took Mattie to the beach on Sunday. They found a car park, which was always a good sign, and the surf was not too rough. After their swim, they strolled along the sand, picking up shells and paddling in the shallows.

"It's nice at the beach, isn't it, Mum? We should do this more often."

"We should," Angela agreed. "When the weather's fine, we'll do it more, I promise."

The surging waves washed between their toes, causing them both to laugh at the buffeting. Looking up from the foamy froth, Angela froze. A previous Mr Tuesday was coming in their direction.

"Time to turn around, Mattie. It might start to get cold."

From over her shoulder, she saw the man had dropped his towel on the sand and was about to head into the water. He was a regular client until the middle of last year. Shortly after he cancelled his booking, with a generous tip on his last afternoon, she'd seen his wedding reported in the social pages. She mentally wished him all the best for his new life. Hopefully, he'd learnt some important lessons, and picked up tips on satisfying his new wife. He was with her now, and she noted evidence of the woman's pregnancy. Good luck to them.

At the beginning of their contact, Mr Tuesday past had been all enthusiasm and no technique. She'd made him stop and then start again, teaching him the nuances and subtleties of how to please a woman and then keep on pleasing her. The improvement was most gratifying. He wasn't and never would be a ten out of ten, but was significantly better than the three out of ten which was her initial rating. His wife would have no idea how much she had Angelique to thank for—and Angela would make sure she never did. She and Mattie did an abrupt turn and headed back in the direction from which they'd come.

"Mum, can we have fish and chips… ple-e-ease?"

"I think we might do that. Can't go to the beach without fish and chips, can we?"

They sat on the sea wall, watching the waves and warding off marauding sea gulls. Every so often, Mattie would throw a chip in the air, giggling as a screeching, feathered mass rose to snatch it before it hit the ground. The sea breezes were sweeping in and the temperature was dropping when they packed up their beach bags and headed back to the car. Mattie was asleep long before they reached home.

With tea, bath and bed sorted, Angela turned out the light in Mattie's room and re-opened her laptop. She wanted to review her portfolio and decide if she needed to make any adjustments for the coming week. She also wanted to investigate the information on Johnson Hydrology. She was thinking of investing in those shares but wasn't sure if her decision was based on rational or emotional reasoning.

She logged on and studied the website, clicking first on the 'About Us' page. Luke Johnson looked back at her, his penetrating gaze one that spoke of professionalism and reliability. Even in his business suit and carefully considered pose, she was aware of the x-factor exuded by the man. It was not quite the view she was accustomed to seeing. She imagined him in his glorious naked state, gazing at her with a look fuelled by lust and desire. Probably not appropriate for a corporate website. She giggled to herself at the mental image before cruising to other sections of the site.

She read the corporate pages, and then searched for alternative business commentary about the business, looking for other analysis and points of view. She would ask Mr Wednesday – in a roundabout way of course. He could advise her, and she respected his opinion. With that decision made, she shut down her files and headed for bed. Tomorrow was the start of another week. Soon it would be Thursday.

2 – Start of the Week

"Sasha, I haven't forgotten. I'll be there. Expecting anyone interesting?" With the phone clutched under her chin, she rinsed off the breakfast dishes at the sink before stacking them in the dishwasher. Multitasking helped her get through the morning chores before Jimmy's arrival.

"Are you looking for new clients?" Sasha countered.

"Not at all. My diary's full. There's no indication anyone's about to move on—or get married. I just wondered who to expect, that's all. I'll do some background research on the guest list this morning before Mr Monday arrives."

Angela could hear the rustle of paper. Sasha still maintained a paper-based diary, liking the easy reference to her key data. She rattled off names and either positions or occupations. There were some captains of industry, a senior banker, and a couple of politicians from either side of the house.

"There will be a few others, but you'll already know them. Tanya McNeil is coming as well. She's just finished a season with the National Opera Company. I'm hoping I might prevail upon her to sing for us."

"You mean you're expecting her to sing for her supper?"

"Don't be silly. Of course not."

Sasha's disapproval of the suggestion was palpable, but Angela knew the woman had a way of getting people to do what she wanted. After all, *she* was attending the soiree; to refuse was not really an option. Sasha liked her guests to feel comfortable, and Angela would be expected to mingle and schmooze, ensuring there were no awkward gaps in conversation. She always picked up the odd piece of strategically important information at these events, and it didn't hurt to lay the groundwork with any prospective clients. You never knew when circumstances might change.

The call ended with pleasantries and Angela's promise to be early the next evening. A ping on her phone indicated Jimmy was waiting for her. She grabbed her bag and the list Sasha had outlined, and ran out to the car, slamming the door behind her.

"Morning Jimmy. Another beautiful week ahead."

"Absolutely, Miss Angelique. Anything or anyone new I should know about?"

"Nobody new, but I need a seafood platter for when Mr Monday arrives later today. He put in a special request, and who am I to deny an Olympic swimmer his aquatic pleasures? Can you take care of that for me?"

They followed the usual routine on arrival at the apartment. Angela didn't exit the car until the grill to the carpark was closed, and Jimmy watched until she had entered the elevator. Seating herself in her office, Angela reviewed the list Sasha had given her. The soiree wasn't until Tuesday evening, but she decided to use her morning to research the names. If she knew what business deals were in the wind, or whose operations were under threat, she would have an idea of which topics to either raise or avoid. Sometimes she would target specific people if she thought they may have market intelligence to her advantage. She had a lot to thank Sasha and Renato for, and strategy was one of them.

By the time Jimmy delivered the platter to the apartment, she had tidied the office and changed into her working clothes. There was no hint of Angela to be seen. After depositing the platter in the kitchen, Jimmy paused in front of a window, hands on hips, admiring the sea view below.

"Great, isn't it? I can almost see my place from here."

He hesitated, and then cleared his throat. Angela sensed it wasn't just the vista that was on his mind. She waited, trying not to look at her watch. It was almost time for her guest.

"Has Mr Monday changed his car?" he asked finally.

"Not that I know of. Why?"

"It's nothing really. There's been a Volvo with dark windows in the street outside and from all I can see, there is no reason for it to be there. It looks like a car that followed us for a while this morning but that might have been a coincidence. I'll keep an eye on it but it's probably my overactive imagination."

Angela knew Jimmy was security-conscious, but surely this was over-reacting? The car couldn't have been there very long. "I'll sound out my visitor and let you know. I can't imagine he'd be parked there early. Paparazzi perhaps, but why would they stake out this street? He's gone to great lengths to keep his visits a secret. Imagine what the media would make of that!"

The buzzer sounded to indicate that Mr Monday was downstairs, and with a shrug and a wink, Jimmy took his leave. Moments later, she greeted her guest with a light kiss and took his coat.

"Come in. Make yourself comfortable. How's the world of Australian Sports?"

"Buzzing as usual. Fortunately, the role takes me out of the office a fair bit. You know me—I go crazy if I'm anchored to a desk. I've just come from a meeting with a major tech company. Hopefully, they're going to provide some sponsorship for junior swimmers next year."

"Well, if anyone can swing the deal, you can. You're like a shark in the water, snapping up everyone in your way."

He laughed, rubbing his hands together in a sign of his nervous energy. "I never thought of it quite like that but yes, I like to win. It's brought me opportunities I never thought possible, without having to follow a black line either!"

"So—are you hungry?"

"Absolutely, but not for prawns just yet. I've a feeling I'm not going to need the oysters either." Wearing a grin that exuded boyish charm, he advanced upon her and with hands clamped on her buttocks, nibbled on her neck. "I was thinking of you and what I wanted to do with you all through that meeting. They thought my look of serious concentration indicated my deep interest in their technical brilliance. Little did they know what was really on my mind."

Given the media profile of Mr Monday, and the number of gorgeous young women who were regularly seen on his arm, Angelique thought they might in fact have a very good idea.

Disentangling herself from his embrace, she led him to the bedroom. Her voice dropped to a huskier register, and she sashayed rather than walked. "Why don't we take care of one appetite first and then we'll address the other."

He was the youngest of her clients, and the one she most likened to a cute but undisciplined puppy. He was off the starting block in a flash. Not one for extended foreplay, he tended to focus on the main event—from his perspective, anyway. Angelique placed a firm hand on his chest and pushed him back onto the bed beside her.

"Easy, Sunshine; this is not a one-horse race, you know. We'll get to the winning post, but this is one event we don't have to win. Why don't you lie back and practice your deep breathing techniques while I show you what a little discipline and self-restraint is like."

He groaned. "I know, Angelique, I know. It's your fault: that's the effect you have on me. Sometimes I get carried away. Slap me around if you need to." He grinned at her lasciviously. "Sometimes I enjoy that too."

Angela tried not to roll her eyes too obviously. She proceeded to tantalise and tease with tongue and fingers, all the while instructing him not to move. She slid down his body, her hardened nipples caressing his chest, and then his stomach. He moaned in ecstasy, his body giving involuntary spasms as she worked her magic.

"Now it's my turn. Show me what you can do."

He started with her feet, knowing from past experience she loved a foot massage. Angela moaned in ecstasy as he dug his knuckles into the balls of her feet, before progressing to suck on her toes with his tongue doing an erotic dance all of its own. She laid back, eyes closed and fingers digging into the surface of the bed, savouring the exquisite sensations. For what Mr Monday paid, the expectation was all about the pleasure he received, but surely there was pleasure in giving as well as receiving?

He worked his way up her inner right leg, and instinctively she spread her limbs wider, ready to receive him. He didn't oblige. With an example of remarkable restraint, he shimmied up the bed to nibble in the hollow at the base of her neck. Her breathing became more ragged and she arched her back, thrusting the peaks of her breasts upwards with each inhalation.

He couldn't fail to notice. The pebble-hard peaks screamed for attention. With the fingers of one hand delicately teasing one nipple, his tongue teased the other. Angela buried her hands in his hair, her fingers grasping those golden locks and the deep breaths gave way to small mewls of pleasure.

There came a time when youthful enthusiasm couldn't be contained any longer., and plunged deep within her, giving a joyous shout as he crossed the finishing line.

With a brief recovery that reflected his level of fitness, he was ready for the next course—or at least for the seafood.

Clad in soft towelling robes, they sat on the balcony with the platter on the table between them. A gentle breeze swept up from the bay, but did nothing to diminish the warm glow of sunshine. It carried with it the smell of the water and the scent of the local frangipani. Summer was on its way.

"I wonder what the poor people are doing today?" A dribble of juice ran down his chin. He ate as exuberantly as he made love.

"Not eating prawns, I suspect. That reminds me, I'm contemplating buying a new car. What are you driving these days?"

"A Toyota Lexus. It's a sponsorship deal, so I have to drive it." He licked his fingers before taking a sip of crisp white. "They upgrade me to the latest model every year."

"So, you've never thought about a Volvo then?"

"Me? Nah—Volvo's are for old farts and I'm not one of them yet."

Later, she reported the conversation to Jimmy. He snorted as she relayed the comments, but reassured her. "I didn't see the car this afternoon, so whoever was driving it has gone. Probably just a local visitor."

Probably was, Jimmy. You'll be checking under the bed next. She didn't dare voice that thought aloud.

Tuesday morning did not start well.

"I feel sick. I don't want to go to school today." Mattie was clearly out of sorts. He'd had disturbed sleep and it showed. He dragged his feet and took forever to get dressed, even after she'd growled at him in exasperation.

"There's nothing wrong with you that a good night's sleep won't fix. It's early bed for you tonight, young man."

"Why can't I stay home today? I really am sick, Mum."

Angela felt a familiar ache in the pit of her belly. She hated these conversations. "I have to go to work, that's why. This is Nan's volunteering day so there's no one to look after you. School it is."

"It's not fair—why do you have to work? Robbie's mum stays home. Why can't you?"

Not for the first time, Angela considered the complications of her work. It would be impossible to take Mattie to the apartment with her. Her clients might take issue with a child sitting in the corner with a tower of Lego, and how could she explain to him what she was doing? The beginnings of a pressure headache lurked behind her eyes. She turned to her pouting son. The situation had to be turned around quickly. A glance at the kitchen clock reminded her Jimmy would be arriving soon.

"Robbie's dad works so his mum can stay home. I'm sorry, Mattie but we don't have a dad living with us. That means I have to work." This conversation always hurt. She squatted down at the same level as her son. "I have to go out this evening, but tomorrow night we could go out for pizza, but only if you're well enough of course."

"Really? Can we go to Mario's? He makes the best!"

"I reckon we could." Angela was relieved at the shift in his spirits. "C'mon—grab your school bag. We'll be late."

She had a bit to think about as she settled into her morning routine at the apartment. Would it be possible to bring forward her career change? She needed to review her financial situation again. Renato could check some of her projections to see if she was over-estimating. If it was achievable, she could spend more time with Mattie, or at least let him stay home from school when he was sick. It would give her the option of some work-life balance as well.

She was better placed financially now than she had been eight years ago, when her dickhead of a husband disappeared. Matthew was only a newborn. Angela had been devastated, and left in dire financial circumstances but had learnt a hard lesson. Never depend on any man, and she hadn't since then. Initially, she'd been employed as bookkeeper and PA to Sasha Berkowitz, a woman with an interesting past of her own.

It was at Sasha's suggestion and with her mentorship that she'd developed her professional services, and put herself on a sound financial footing. Now it was time to look for an alternative business opportunity, one which allowed her to operate above the public radar. Most importantly, it needed to be a business that gave her more flexibility in relation to Mattie.

She did have an idea. It was kind of crazy and only half-formed. She rang her mentor to get her view.

"Morning Sasha. I know you're busy with preparations for this evening, but I want to run something past you."

She explained her morning conversation with Matthew. "It's time to start considering my next move. The investments are helpful but it will be a long time before I can rely on them. I need an alternative business, one that's more kid-friendly."

"That could be a challenge." Sasha's acknowledgement of this statement was non-committal. She and Renato, who had married late, well after Sasha had secured her own financial security, had never had children, so taking them into account had not been required.

Angela pushed on. "You and Renato have given me such sound advice. If it weren't for you, I'd still be struggling to survive on a bookkeeper's salary. I need to keep earning, but my current activities are short term only. I'm thinking about what's next."

"Very wise. What do you have in mind? I assume you've come up with an idea." Her voice betrayed her curiosity.

"You know me too well. The idea came to me last week while I was having my nails done. The salon I use is fairly run down but the location is brilliant. The woman who owns it is pregnant and mentioned in passing that with the new baby coming, she'd really like to spend more time with her family. I'm thinking of making an offer for the business."

"But you're not a beautician. You don't know anything about the business." Sasha's incredulous tone indicated her thoughts on the concept.

"I can soon learn, though I wouldn't be hands-on in that sense. I'd give the establishment a make-over, and employ some top technicians in that field. I have in mind an up-market salon, and at my opening night, would invite some of the women I've met in recent years. It hasn't all been about the men, you know. I've met some fascinating women at your soirees as well. This would be a place where women of style and class would come to be pampered. Once the first salon was established, I'd look at strategic locations for the next. It would be the place to be seen. What do you think?"

There was a moment's silence, while Sasha digested the concept. "Are you sure you're ready to take this step? You're doing so well at the moment. Establishing a new business will take both time and money. I'm not saying it isn't a good idea, but you need to do some research before committing yourself."

"Sure. I'm not going to rush into this, but I think, in fairness to Matthew, I need to make myself ready. This current work has been a fabulous opportunity, but it's time to consider the future."

"If that's the case, I might be able to help you. A guest attending this evening owns a distribution business that supplies the beauty industry. He and I go way back. I'll ask him to come early and you can have a chat to him. I'm sure he'll be most helpful. He can advise you on industry trends, and potential competitors. I'll confirm with you after I've spoken to him."

It was a plan. Angela felt the weight of indecision lift as she terminated the call and made a list of things she needed to investigate. She opened a notebook and searched in the bottom of her bag for her favourite pen. She needed it for something so important. *Review of assets and liabilities, identify industry competitors, market rental rates, services in hot demand...* Lists made her feel better. They made her feel under control and being in control was important. She was relieved as well to have the support of her mentor. It gave her greater confidence in her forward planning.

Angela's phone rang with the distinctive tone that indicated Jimmy was calling. Looking up from the current investment module, she welcomed the distraction. Her head spun after trying to grasp the finer points of short trading and then alternatively trading long.

"Hi Jimmy."

"I'm a bit concerned about Mr Tuesday."

"Why? What's happened?"

"Nothing serious, but that car's parked outside again. Maybe he's the focus. There's something about it that has my nose twitching. Do you think he's on someone's radar—some foreign power perhaps?"

"Jimmy, I think you've been watching too many movies. You know he's very careful. He insisted on his own minder doing a sweep of the apartment before he even set foot inside. It's the only time I've allowed an external person in here, aside from the clients."

"Yeah, I know. I'd hate anything to happen on my watch. Just thought I'd let you know."

"Thanks. I always feel secure knowing you've got my back. I should tell you more often how much I appreciate you."

"Just doin' my job, Miss Angelique. That's what you pay me for."

Angela flicked to the online news after finishing the call. Mr Tuesday was reported holding a press conference about a major contract negotiated on behalf of the Defence Department. There had been interviews on the radio that morning as well. She and Jimmy had listened to them during the morning commute. Mr Tuesday was under a lot of pressure at the moment, but he seemed to thrive on that, having a well-oiled machine around him to take care of some of life's more mundane chores. As she noted with a touch of irony, even sex was also outsourced.

Angela wondered what investigations he might have initiated about her, and what he had managed to find out. She was protective about her private life and minimised her digital footprint as much as possible. In spite of that, she wasn't so naïve as to think that a determined professional wouldn't turn up some information.

Mr Tuesday was on time. To the second. That was unusual for him, as he was often held up by matters of state. Whenever that occurred, one of his trusted minders would call her to advise of the delay.

He threw off his jacket and loosened his tie as he came through the door.

"Busy day?" Angelique asked as she picked up the jacket and hung it up.

"You've no idea! I could kill for a cup of coffee."

"Coming right up." She made a small pot of coffee with his preferred single-origin blend. "I heard you on the radio this morning," she added by way of conversation. "It sounded as though some tough negotiating has been going on behind the scenes."

"It has been," he agreed, "but you have to know when to play the waiting game. It paid off in the end."

While he talked, Angelique massaged his shoulders, feeling the tight knots under his fingers. "You need to do something about the stress you're carrying."

"I am. What do you think I'm doing here?" He gave her a quick smile, and in that instant the tiredness seemed to ease from his face. It was a boyish look, in spite of the thinning hair and receding hairline, with an indication of what he must have looked like in earlier years. "A couple of hours here with you and it feels like I've had a week in a spa."

She threw back her head and laughed; a deep, throaty, joyful laugh. "That's the nicest thing anyone's said to me in a while."

As it turned out, they didn't progress to the bedroom. This was one of those occasions when he was happy to just talk, though he did have a little snooze after she finished with his shoulders. For the first time he talked about his family and some of the concerns he had with his teenage sons. Angelique never asked about her client's private lives, but if they chose to talk, then she listened. They knew the conversation never left the apartment. She didn't volunteer information about her private life, and if questions were asked, she had some stock responses prepared.

My life is rather boring. I'm more interested in you.

Oh, just the usual—mundane childhood, left school early... I'm just a girl trying to get ahead. How did you get your start in life?

I'd rather talk about you. You've made such an impression in the world of commerce/politics/society.

They soon learned not to ask.

He left in a more relaxed state than when he arrived, though his phone started vibrating furiously when he switched it back on at the door. With a quick kiss, Mr Tuesday was gone, summonsed by matters that helped keep the country running.

It was a while before Jimmy spoke when he picked her up later that afternoon. He kept looking in the rear vision mirror.

"It was there again, Miss Angelique. I've scoped out the street and I'm sure it's not associated with anyone who lives or works here. It can't be Mr Monday who's drawn their interest. Perhaps you should warn Mr Tuesday."

It took her a moment to realise he was talking about the Volvo again.

"If it's still there tomorrow, I'll call him. I mean—we don't have any evidence, do we? It's just a suspicion."

"When you've been around as long as I have, you learn to pay attention to your suspicions. He's a very important man. I'd hate to see him fall into the wrong hands."

"You're right Jimmy. I'll call him tomorrow." She checked her watch. There was no time to worry about it now. "I've got a function on at Sasha's tonight and I need to get Mattie organised before I go. My mother will look after him. Can you pick me up again at seven?"

By the time Jimmy returned, Matthew was fed and bathed and was having a story read to him by his grandmother. Angela gave them both a kiss, mentioned there was ice cream in the freezer, and headed out to the car. She'd managed to tame her long hair into a sleek up-do, which showed off her diamond drop earrings to perfection. They were her only adornment. She operated on the principle that less was more. Her dress of midnight blue satin was styled in a simple sheath, with a bateau neckline sitting just off her shoulders. The smooth satiny skin of her décolletage didn't need further enhancement. On impulse, she added a dash of her favourite perfume to her cleavage, then ran out to meet Jimmy at the car.

The Berkowitz house, with an impressive stone façade, was built over three levels. The ground floor consisted of the public rooms, including the salon. This was a large room in which Sasha and Renato did their major entertaining and it opened onto the rear of the dwelling, with French doors leading onto the terrace and the manicured garden beyond. There was a smaller room towards the front of the house that was used for more intimate entertaining or discussions.

Although Sasha and Renato were private people and discrete with their business dealings, in the circles that mattered, an invitation to one of these soirees was keenly sought. It was recognition of status for those for whom these things were important. Sasha managed that reputation carefully.

Renato met Angela at the door. "Angelique, my dear. How delightful you look tonight. Sasha is in the kitchen checking the catering details. Sheldon Weybourne is already here. Come through."

Renato kissed her cheek and led her into the salon. Angela was genuinely fond of the man. She had never known her father, and Renato filled a de facto parental role.

"How are your studies coming on?" he enquired. It was Renato who suggested she acquire more structured knowledge of the financial markets. He was always ready with advice, but insisted she needed a greater understanding herself if she was to become a successful investor.

"Good—I think. Some of it gets a bit overwhelming. I might make a time to sit with you and discuss the aspects I don't fully understand. I'm sure you can put it in simple terms for me."

"I'd be delighted to help. Can I fetch you a drink?"

She requested her usual—mineral water in a champagne glass with a single drop of grenadine. It looked like pink champagne and kept her head clear for the evening. The night was all about business, not getting tipsy though she might indulge in the real thing later.

The man waiting in the salon was well-dressed, in a suit that spoke of a tailored fit, and wearing polished leather shoes that were probably handmade. His dark hair was brushed back, with streaks of distinguished grey at the temples, giving some indication as to his age. His trim body suggested he spent time at the gym—either that or his metabolism was kind to him.

Renato made the introductions and fetched them both the drink of their choice. Sheldon offered a firm handshake, and Angela noted the smooth skin. Perhaps he used his own skincare products. As she observed the man introduced to her, she wondered if he had been a client of Sasha's in the early days. If so, he must have passed her muster. When attending events hosted by Sasha, she often surveyed the attending men and wondered which of them knew Sasha a little better than others.

She became aware that a pair of observant blue eyes were regarding her just as intently.

"Delighted to meet you, Angelique. Sasha has told me so much about you."

She smiled politely in response, wondering just what Sasha had said. "Well, you're one up on me. Sasha hasn't told me much about you at all, except that you operate a supply business for the beauty trade and you might be able to give me some good advice about buying into that industry."

His genuine smile reached all the way to the crinkles at the corner of his eyes. "In that case she told you all you really need to know, but I'm sure I'll fill in some more detail as we talk. Explain to me first what your objectives are and what you're hoping to get from the industry that you're not getting elsewhere."

Sasha bustled in from the kitchen. She greeted Angela with a kiss on each cheek, and Sheldon with a kiss on the lips.

"Two of my favourite people! Before you two get engrossed, you might like to adjourn to my office. That will be more private if other guests are inconsiderate enough to arrive early."

She led them to a meeting table in the room used as her office and left them to their discussion. The room had been stylishly furnished by Sasha's favourite designer, but was clearly a work environment. Drapes in peach silk were tied to the sides of the bay window, and the window seat was upholstered in matching velvet. The white marble mantelpiece over the fireplace supported a vase of magnificent creamy roses, reflected in the gilt-edged mirror hanging above.

Aware of the limited time, they got down to business. Sheldon sat, one leg crossed over the other as he leaned back on his chair, an arm slung over the back and gesturing expressively with the other. "Let's get started. Shall we begin with current trends?" he asked.

"Yes, please," Angela replied.

"Fabulous." He sipped his drink and launched into a description of the current economic climate and the implications for business.

Angela scribbled in her notebook brought with her for the purpose, trying to keep up as Sheldon jumped from one topic to the next. He described current trends, demographic and cultural influences and told her the background to his foray into the beauty industry. It had been due to the involvement of his grandmother, a beautician who had worked her way up from being employed in a salon, to owning it. Sheldon had initially trained as an accountant, working for a major corporation. Realising that environment was not for him, he took over financial management of his grandmother's business, and eventually took over the running of it as well.

"You have to like people to succeed in this business, Angelique. Our operation has changed over the years so now I deal with salons rather than the clients who patronise them, but this much I do know. People skills are essential."

"I think I have a few of those," Angela responded. There was no need to elaborate. "What are the popular services people are seeking today? I was assuming hair removal, anti-ageing treatment and a range of skin therapies would be high on the list."

"All of that, plus natural therapy modalities. You would need the latest in therapeutic equipment and be able to provide skilled technicians. I'll speak to Wendy, my operations manager. If you're interested, you could accompany her as she does her rounds. She regularly visits our client salons and she can give you more of the hands-on detail. Make some time to chat to me after that, and I'll give you an idea of expected profit margins and operating costs as best I know them."

"Sheldon, that's most generous of you. I would really appreciate the opportunity if Wendy is agreeable. It would help me make up my mind."

"My pleasure. Any friend of Sasha's is a friend of mine. I think Wendy will be visiting salons in the morning, if that's not too soon for you."

"As long as I can confine it to the morning, that should be fine. I have an afternoon commitment."

Sheldon called Wendy and put the arrangements in place. The operations manager would pick Angela up at nine the following morning. Muffled voices indicated other guests were arriving. They wrapped up their discussion, and went to join them.

Angela's head was buzzing with options and possibilities, but she put those thoughts aside and focussed on more social matters. She mingled, greeting those she knew and introducing herself to those she didn't. She made sure no-one was left on the outer, and helped the conversation along when it appeared to be floundering. That didn't happen often in a crowd like this.

The function was one hour in when Sasha introduced Tanya McNeil to the guests. The event was running smoothly, and Angela felt she could finally relax. Her discussions with Sheldon had been fruitful and she had met her obligations with Sasha. She surveyed the room again, making sure she hadn't missed anyone important.

"Good evening. How delightful to see you here, Angelique."

The voice came from behind her, but she didn't need to turn around to know who it was. Her heart lurched so violently she felt physically shocked. Composing her face to hide her emotions, she turned to face him. She hoped the flush she could feel didn't betray her.

Mr Thursday stood before her, looking more debonair in his dinner suit than she was accustomed to seeing him.

3 – The Soiree

"I wasn't expecting to see you this evening." It was silly not to, given this was where she had first met him.

"Is that a problem?" He raised one eyebrow in query.

"Not at all—sorry, that sounded rude." She mentally pulled herself together. It was important she handle this right. "Of course, I'm delighted to see you." *You've no idea how delighted I am.* She could already feel a warm sensual rush between her thighs. The smile she directed to him was open, with sultry overtones as she struggled to regain her composure.

"I'm reassured to hear it. Looking around, I see we're in rather important company. Do you know Sasha and Renato well?"

"Well enough. They're old friends and have been good to me over the years. Do you have a drink? I'd get one now if I were you. I think Tanya McNeil is about to sing."

Diverting the conversation away from sensitive areas was an old strategy. She caught the attention of the drinks waiter and took a champagne flute from his tray, handing it to her companion. On impulse, she took another for herself. It was time for some fortification.

He downed half the glass in one swallow. "Do you know except for when we first met, you've never called me by my name? Why is that? It would be nice if you did occasionally. It would make me feel I was more of a real person to you, rather than…"

He trailed off, leaving a meaningful silence. Angela felt herself colouring again. Referring to her clients by the relevant days was a useful strategy in maintaining a professional distance, but she didn't do that to their face. Of all her clients, Lucas Johnson was the one who made her wish that things were different.

"You don't have to call me Lucas," he added. "Most people call me Luke. I'm okay with that."

"Sure—Luke." She held his gaze, mischievously.

The pianist, engaged for the occasion, began his opening chords. Tanya positioned herself by his side, ready for her opening cue. Luke grasped Angela's arm and pulled her towards the French doors leading to the terrace and the night air.

"If we stay inside, we'll never hear ourselves talk. We'll appreciate her beautiful voice just as easily from the garden."

It was a mild night and for that Angela was grateful. She hadn't brought a wrap with her. They had the terrace to themselves, other guests having wandered back inside for the recital. Still holding her arm, Luke stopped, turning to face her.

"That perfume smells exquisite. Very you. In my mind, I'm seeing you wearing that perfume and little else—except for those earrings."

"I'll take that on notice. It's not Thursday."

"Does it have to be?"

"That was the agreement; yes it does."

Angela didn't want to say she had clients booked on the other days of the week. He must realise but she wasn't going to flaunt the fact. She looked meaningfully at her arm and he released his grip. The imprint of his fingers remained, a memento of his touch.

His look became one of speculation. "I've got a suggestion. Do you have a passport?"

"Yes, but I don't plan on going anywhere." Her heartbeat speeded up a pace. Where was this going?

"But you could do. I need to travel to the Middle East to showcase some hydro-technologies at the end of next week. You could come with me, all expenses paid of course." Reaching out, he slid a finger down the side of her face, his touch feather-light. The powerful voice of Tanya McNeil swirled around them as Angela regarded him, a million thoughts in her head. It was such a tantalizing idea, spending more than an afternoon in his company. She couldn't leave Mattie though and how would she explain going away to her mother?

There was another thing bothering her. He was looking on her as his sexual companion and that wasn't what she wanted at all. She wanted to be so much more, if only that were an option. It would be naïve to think it was. She'd fantasised about it often enough, but there were times when your head had to overrule your heart.

"Sweet offer," she said in a voice that was huskier than she meant it to be, "but it wouldn't be possible. I have commitments here I have to meet."

"Are you sure? Just cancel them."

In the soft light on the patio, his eyes looked like pools of dark chocolate and twice as rich. Their effect was scorching; she could feel her inner core melting. She wanted him to keep touching her, not just her face but all of her. She dropped her eyes to release herself from their power.

"You don't just click your fingers at me and expect me to come running," she said stiffly, trying hard to mask her feelings.

"Perhaps that's what's so appealing—that and other things. Surely with a couple of weeks' notice, you can make arrangements."

"Some things can't be changed. Enticing idea, but I do have significant commitments."

He regarded her for a moment. "You mean like your son, for instance?"

Her head jerked up. She pulled away from his touch. Her emotions turned to ice in an instant. "What are you talking about?"

"Not what; who. I understand you have a young son. Arrangements can be made for his care while you're away."

Panic threatened to choke her. She'd never told him about Matthew, or told any of her clients for that matter. Her personal life was exactly that. "Who suggested I have a child?"

"You don't think I enter into any relationship, business or otherwise, without doing my research, do you? I call it risk management. I learn what I can about those with whom I'm involved." He paused to sip his champagne, maintaining eye contact over the rim of his glass. "I'm sure an astute woman such as yourself does the same."

"And just what did you learn about me?" It was an effort not to sound shrill.

"You'd be surprised. It's difficult to hide in this digital day and age. I started with a title search on your apartment and then followed with a company search to uncover who was behind the entity that owned it. I fell down a few rabbit holes but I have good people working for me who have this sort of research down to a fine art."

Are all the clients doing this level of research? Have I been fooling myself all along and my life has been an open book?

"And what do you do with this information you uncover?"

Her face must have registered her distress, as he removed her champagne flute from her grasp and put it along with his on the patio table. Seizing her by the arms, he pulled her close. The scent of his cologne, which previously had been tantalising now threatened to overwhelm. She wanted to pull away.

"I do nothing with it. It's for my benefit alone. As I said, it's risk management and unless a high-risk event occurs, nobody else need ever know about it. I've never had the impression that you pose a risk. Far from it."

"Why don't I feel reassured?"

"Are you saying you haven't undertaken research on me? Have you let me into your life in the way you have without undertaking some form of due diligence?"

That sounded so much like a business transaction, which if she was honest, it was. She had to quell the bitterness in her thoughts. Angela had done her own research, but she was not going to admit that. It would only give tacit approval to his actions. Time to return inside.

"Thank you for your kind invitation," she replied stiffly, "but I have to decline. It's time to join the other guests. Sasha and Renato will think I've abandoned them."

Shaking off his grip, she fled for the safety of the salon, not looking to see if he was following. She hoped he wasn't. She needed time to process what she'd learned. She grabbed a fresh drink from a waiter and with a smile firmly plastered, set about the schmoozing that was expected, conscious of his gaze following her. It was difficult not to be aware of him, even when talking to other people.

He didn't approach her again until the end of the evening. She was backed into a corner at the time with a foreign diplomat who was leering into her cleavage.

"Angelique," Luke exclaimed, "I need to catch up with you before I leave."

He nodded politely at the diplomat, and inserted himself, initially to their side, but progressively easing himself between them.

"We didn't have the opportunity to finish our earlier conversation," he said, his eyes wide and guileless. "Wasn't Tanya McNeil wonderful? I could listen to a voice like hers all night."

He gradually turned his back towards the diplomat. That gentleman finally left, muttering something under his breath, which although not audible, did not sound at all complimentary.

"I didn't need rescuing."

"I'm sure you can look after yourself," he replied smoothly, "but he's such a bore. Besides, I didn't want to leave things as they were when we spoke earlier. I wanted to assure you that I have no puerile interest in your private life. I needed to understand what I was getting myself into and with whom. There's a lot more I would like to know about you if you would only give me the opportunity."

He dropped his voice a level, and the intensity of the look he gave her would melt an iceberg. It threatened to melt more than that. He fished a card from his wallet. "I know you have my contact details, but the number on this card is my private number and you can reach me on that at any time. If you change your mind about going away, give me a call. If you change your mind about anything, give me a call."

He leant forward and softly kissed her cheek before turning to leave. It was only as he reached the door of the salon that he turned and called softly, "See you Thursday," and with that he was gone.

Angela felt inexplicably abandoned. To see him had been an unexpected thrill. His disclosure had floored her and she needed time to consider the implications. Now, she didn't want him to go and was confused by her feelings. It was easier not to think about him at all. There was no point.

After other guests had left, she sat with Sasha and Renato, shoes off and cup of tea in hand.

"A good evening, I think," Renato commented. "Learn anything interesting, my dear?"

Ever the astute investor, he often acquired interesting snippets of information that complemented or directed his market research and had previously advised her to follow suit.

"Perhaps. There was a diverse group of people here this evening. I always find someone interesting to talk to."

"I noticed you talking to Luke Johnson. Be careful, Angela. It can be a mistake to mix business with pleasure." Sasha's pursed lips indicated a measure of caution.

"But Sasha, pleasure is my business—where Luke Johnson is concerned anyway." She couldn't help but laugh. "I know what you mean though. He invited me to go on an overseas trip with him. I refused of course." She couldn't hide the regret in her voice.

"He's a fine-looking man," Renato acknowledged, "and an astute businessman as well. I've been monitoring his operations for some time. The company's doing interesting things in the area of water delivery to remote locations. He is a man with a social conscience, and I like that."

"That's all very well," interrupted Sasha, "but you have a plan, Angela, and you're so close to meeting your financial objectives. Don't do anything to threaten that now."

"So, was your meeting with Sheldon productive?" inquired Renato. "Did he offer any useful information?"

Ever the diplomat, he always knew when to divert the conversation. Angela flicked him a quick smile of gratitude. "Yes, it was brilliant. I'm meeting with his Operations Manager tomorrow, and she's going to take me on her rounds during the morning. I know these are early days, but this might be a practical option for me. Thank you so much for the introduction."

"I thought Sheldon would be a good contact," Sasha commented. "It's wise to leave your current line of business while you are at your peak; more opportunities are open to you then. Don't shut down operations though until you have adequate cash reserves and a clear business plan for what you will do next. Investment returns can be unreliable. Make sure you have your safety net in place."

"You're right, I know," Angela sighed. "I don't mind the work—it has some pleasurable moments—but it's not my forever job. I want to quit before Matthew gets old enough to start asking questions. I'm amazed that my mother still believes I'm your bookkeeper and personal assistant."

Sasha smiled. "Sometimes, a mother knows when not to ask too many questions. Seriously though, don't make any rash decisions, and keep your gentlemen wanting more. Don't let any of them get too involved. It's an unnecessary complication."

~

Luke cursed to himself as he drove away from the event. He'd hoped Angelique would be there. That was the main reason he'd accepted the invitation and he'd blown it. He was crazy to let a woman like her get under his skin; he was just a client, after all. Logic told him he wasn't the only one, but he didn't want to go there.

Frustratingly for a man who pulled all the strings in his life, Angelique made him feel like a teenager again—full of angst and uncontrollable lustful desire. When he saw her in that dress revealing the creamy skin of her shoulders and décolletage, it did more for him than if she'd been standing there stark naked.

Things had been going so well; she'd seemed genuinely pleased to see him. More than anything, he wanted the opportunity to get to know the woman away from the waterfront apartment and in a totally different context. Taking her with him on his work trip had seemed one way of achieving that, and then he would have had a measure of control over the situation.

He should have known better than to mention her son, and the fact he'd researched her background. As soon as he saw the fleeting expression of horror, he knew he'd seriously undermined any gains he'd made in getting to know her better.

And you pride yourself on being a good negotiator, he chided himself. *You don't even rate a mention in these stakes.*

Somehow, he had to come up with a way to repair the damage he'd done but had no idea what that could be.

4 – Wednesday and a Black Volvo

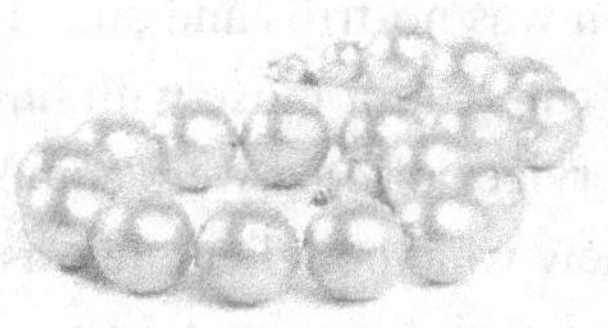

As arranged, Wendy picked Angela up early the next morning. They were only spending a couple of hours together, but it was a welcome change to Angela's financial studies. Wendy was smartly turned out in business attire, and with impeccable grooming. Her handshake was firm.

"You want to learn about this business? You've come to the right place. Sheldon asked me to give you some background, so you could see how the industry operates." She ushered Angela towards the car and unlocked the passenger door before moving around to the driver's side and climbing in. "I'll have to ask if the managers of the two salons we'll be visiting object to your presence, and I may take some conversations in the back room, but otherwise it should be an informative visit."

"I appreciate you accommodating me this way, Wendy. I've a lot to learn before making a firm decision. I promise

I'll be discreet and not intrude on any confidential business discussions."

Angela made the most of their time in the car, interrogating the other woman on trends, market demographics, and whatever else she might know about the fixed outgoings to expect.

The first salon was no-frills and aimed at the city office-worker market. It catered for those with limited time and budget, and the services offered were comprehensive but the salon manager knew what her clientele was prepared to pay. There were defined peak times centred around lunch times and late afternoon and staffing levels were structured around this.

The second salon was in an affluent location, with clientele that was a little more exclusive. Customers featured stay-at-home mothers, retirees, and those working from home. These clients were looking for a little more indulgence and this was reflected in the décor and the types of products that were used. Neither salon quite matched what Angela had in mind, but she found both visits to be informative anyway.

It occurred to Angela that she didn't know much about Wendy's background. She hoped the question wasn't too intrusive. "Wendy, what brought you into this industry?"

"Part circumstance and part necessity. I started off as a beautician, so I understood the client side of the business and got to know Sheldon that way. I'd only worked part time, but when things got a bit tough at home financially, I had to look for fulltime work. It coincided with Sheldon broadening his operations and here I am."

"Are you married?"

"Yes. We're still together, but David has a gambling problem. It imposed a huge financial strain on our marriage. He's a reformed character, but I threatened to divorce him if he ever did it again. It's been such a struggle hiding it from everyone—particularly his workplace. He'd be crucified if they found out."

"Sounds like you've had a tough time. It's under control now?"

"As far as I know, yes it is. I think he's learnt his lesson. You'd think a grown man would know better!"

She didn't hide her bitterness. Angela felt sorry for the woman, but was pleased they were nearly back home. It cut short the awkward conversation and she didn't really want to get involved.

They drew up in Angela's street, with an agreement that Angela would join Wendy again on the following Friday morning. They would visit a couple of salons in a different part of the city.

"Thanks Wendy. You've given me more food for thought, and practical advice to boot. I really appreciate it." Angela waved as the other woman drove off. It had been a very instructive morning. Her notebook was full of suggestions and her mind teemed with possibilities. She could really do this.

Angela and Jimmy travelled to the apartment later in companionable silence, broken only by the radio. It suited her fine. Her mind kept returning to the soiree, and Luke

Johnson. Scattered thoughts threatened to derail her composure. She had to maintain a professional distance from her clients, separating the physical from the emotional. It was part of her survival strategy.

Luke was different. He'd crept under her skin from day one. Just thinking about him made her feel throbbingly wet. What had he learnt about her private life and about Matthew? The realisation he'd successfully investigated her was unnerving. It made her feel vulnerable. Perhaps she should terminate her client relationship with him. Could she really bear to do that?

By the time she arrived at the apartment, she had a headache from over-thinking and didn't feel at all like working. She fantasized about telling Jimmy to keep driving, and to play hooky for the day. She and Matthew were two of a kind.

"Discipline be my middle name," she murmured to herself as she stepped into the elevator. "Just suck it up, sister. It won't be forever."

It was a cooler day, and dark, scudding clouds sat low on the horizon, casting a pall on the bay below. The white sails of yachts on the water stood out in stark relief, but Angela didn't admire the view. She went to her office, sorted the day's mail, and opened her laptop. She had to do some serious number crunching, taking into account the detail that Sheldon and Wendy had given her.

It was only when she stopped for a cup of coffee that she realised it was time to get ready for Mr Wednesday. At least he was a low-stress client. He made her laugh. He reminded her of a large, amiable bear. He was a man who knew how to enjoy himself. He liked good food, he liked good wine, and he liked good sex—in no particular order. He had a generous spirit, and was determined his partner should reach the same giddy pinnacles of joy that he did.

"How's my favourite girl?" He bellowed as he came through the door, enveloping her in a bear hug.

"This woman is great, thank you" she replied pointedly. He just laughed. He'd never succeeded in grasping that such references to grown women were patronising and disrespectful.

"I hope you don't expect girls to provide the sort of services you get with me," Angela added. "There's a name for men like that."

He patted her bottom as he continued into the apartment. "Sweetheart, you could be eighty and you'd still be a girl to me. Have I told you what a wonderfully sexy bottom you've got?"

"Many times, but I'm happy for you to tell me again. It reassures me there's some consistency in my world. I hope I still have a wonderfully sexy bottom at eighty."

He erupted with a great bellowing laugh, one that reeked of confidence in his own humorous interventions.

"Can I get you a drink?" Angela asked.

"Later. I have more pressing needs right now."

The look he gave her was lascivious and hungry. Angela could interpret a cue when she saw one, and led him to the bedroom. She had to slow down his initial exuberance, making him understand there were times in which less was more, and lightness of touch was everything. He was responsive. She didn't expect anything less.

She enjoyed their Wednesday assignations. There was no artifice on his part. He was a financier, holding a senior role in a boutique bank. He oversaw investment strategies and enjoyed sharing his expert knowledge.

"Has that satisfied your initial appetite? I can get you that drink now if you like."

For an answer, he patted her bottom again. "That'd be lovely, Sweetheart."

Angela brought the whiskey and soda back to the bed, plus a soda on the rocks for her. She plumped up the pillows so they could lean back in comfort against the bedhead. The curtains to the bedroom window were drawn wide, allowing them to glimpse the harbour below. It was a relaxing view, and once again, Angela was pleased she'd secured the waterfront apartment.

"So how does a man as busy as you keep up with everything that happens in the world of finance?"

"Delegation; that's the secret. I use good people to do the research and that leaves me time to review the results. I need that clarity if I'm to make key investment decisions."

"Clarity—is that what you get when you visit me?"

He gave a hoot of laughter, his ample belly shaking as a consequence. "I don't think I'd call this clarity, Sweetheart. The term 'mind-blowing' comes to mind. You remind me though there's more to life than work, so you could say that's clarity."

She settled herself more comfortably, flicking the hair back from her face. She trailed a finger down his chest, weaving a path through the curling hairs, dark with flecks of grey. She had the feeling that were it possible for him to purr, he would have done so.

"Even if others do the research, you still need in-depth knowledge to understand what's in their reports. What do you prefer—mining stocks, utilities or new technologies?"

"Diversify, Angelique. You've got to spread your risk."

Angela tried hard not to show her irritation at the patronising response. "And diversification is Investment one-oh-one. That much I understand. What do you think of infrastructure investment? Airports and roads seem to provide a good return, and now you can even invest in power and water services. I'm not so sure how to analyse those companies."

"There can be some promising returns, but I like to see a solid track record first."

"Well, what do you think of Johnson Hydrology for instance?"

"Promising. They've had some good runs on the board, not just in Australia but overseas as well."

"So are they a good investment?"

"Don't hold me to it, but I think they will be. I wouldn't sink everything into their stock, but a few shares would nicely round out a portfolio."

Angela mentally reviewed this information. She would read the company reports again after he'd gone before making a final decision, but she was leaning towards the investment. The question in her mind was whether her interest in the company was influenced by her relationship to Luke, or what she knew of his business. This needed to be a dispassionate decision. In some ways, the two were intertwined – without the business acumen of Luke Johnson, the company would not have achieved its current success. Without that success, he would never have afforded her 'executive coaching services'.

Their conversation meandered onto travel related topics, with Mr Wednesday talking about his most recent trip overseas with his wife, and Angela listening with longing. Her thoughts strayed to the invitation she'd received the night before. To be able to travel in style and with an attentive partner would be fabulous but that was not going to happen—not in the short term anyway. As for the future, one could but dream.

When Mr Wednesday finally took his leave, Angela went through her usual routine of tidying the unit and removing any trace of his presence with a slight spring in her step. Tomorrow was Thursday, and she didn't want any hint of Monday, Tuesday or Wednesday to remain. She wondered if their recent encounter at Sasha's soiree would influence their rendezvous. She also wondered how to find out what he knew about her and if he intended to do anything with that information. It put Luke Johnson in a position of power, and that made her feel insecure. Perhaps Jimmy could advise her.

A ping on her phone let her know Jimmy was waiting for her downstairs. With one last visual check of the apartment, she locked up and took the elevator down to the basement.

"Hi Jimmy. Seen any black Volvos today?"

"Not at all, Miss Angelique. Whoever they were, they must have moved on. Nothing to do with us."

"I'm glad I've got your eyes on the lookout. I would never have noticed them, whether malicious or not."

She still had last night's conversation on her mind. It had plagued her throughout the day. "Jimmy, I wonder if you could do something for me."

"Happy to. Need someone taken care of? I'm your man."

She laughed. "Nothing so dramatic. I want to know what information is available about me, and what someone with intent could find out. I know there'll be costs, and that's not a problem. Call it risk management, if you like. I need to know what others could uncover. Start with doing a title search on this unit and take it from there. I know you'll have resources that might not be available to me."

"I'll get onto it in the morning. Is there any time requirement?"

"No hurry, but can you give me a progress report by the end of the week?"

A message flashed up on the screen of her phone. It was Matthew. He had one of her old phones, but was only allowed to use it at home.

Mum, don't come home.

That was odd – what was he up to? They were almost home anyway, so she'd find out soon enough.

~

As they turned into her street, a vehicle pulled away from the kerb in front of her townhouse.

"That's funny; it's another black Volvo. Might be the season for them. Must be a lot of old farts around."

Jimmy wasn't laughing. "It's not another black Volvo; it's *the* black Volvo. I took note of the registration yesterday. What's it doing here?"

A wave of unease swept over Angela. Could it be coincidental? Somehow, she thought not.

"Jimmy, before you go, I'll just see if Mum noticed anything. Do you mind waiting?"

"I'll come in too. I'll be happier if I check everything's okay."

As they walked up the garden path, the front door flew open, revealing Louise, Angela's mother, and Matthew peering from behind her.

"Angela—thank goodness you're home. Did you see them?"

"See who? What's happened Mum? Who are they?"

"I don't know who they are, and I don't think I want to know. I answered a knock at the door and they just burst in. I thought it was a random home invasion at first, but they knew your name. They thought you were here." Louise sounded on the verge of tears.

"Did they threaten you or hurt you in any way?" interrupted Jimmy.

"We're not hurt, just shaken up."

He looked up and down the street before ushering them all towards the door. "We'd all better go inside while we sort this out. Miss Angelique, I think a cup of tea's in order."

"What did they say?" Angela asked after they'd retreated to the kitchen and the kettle filled. "What did they want?"

"They wanted you, actually. I didn't understand it at all. They said if you didn't give them what they wanted, they'd be back and when they did, they would take Matthew and hold him until you cooperated."

He head swam. Involuntarily, she clutched her chest and her heart giving a protesting thump. "Take Matthew… and he heard that?"

One look at her son's white face told her he'd heard it all.

"He was upstairs in his room initially, but when he heard the raised voices, came out onto the landing."

"I was scared for you, Mum," Matthew said shakily. "That's when I texted you. I was scared you'd come home in the middle of it and then they might have hurt you."

Angela turned to Jimmy in wordless entreaty. Surely there was some mistake? Strange men here? Threatening her Mattie?

He patted her on the arm, but addressed her son. "They won't hurt your mum while I'm around, Matthew. For that matter, I won't let them hurt you either. I'll keep you both safe." With his hands-on-hips stance, Jimmy looked ready to tackle anyone who came near.

Angela turned back to her mother. "So then what happened, Mum?"

"They looked up and saw Matthew, and that's when they made their threat. How could they frighten a small boy like that?"

Louise banged the milk and teapot on the benchtop as she prepared to make the tea. "They wouldn't have had a chance to get near him. I would have flattened them myself before that happened." Her fists were clenched and she looked ready to clock anyone who came within striking distance.

"I know that Mum, but you still haven't said what they wanted. Why did they threaten to take Matthew?"

"They said they knew where you worked, what you did and who you did it with. What did they mean by that? It's no secret that you work for Sasha Berkowitz, is it?" Louise frowned. "They said they've been watching and they want the man who visits you on Fridays. There would be further instructions. If you did as you were told, Matthew would be safe." She paused. "Angela, what's going on? Why do I have the feeling you've been keeping me in the dark about things?"

Angela and Jimmy exchanged a glance. How much to say?

"I'm not sure what they meant, Mum." She turned back to her son. "Matthew, there's nothing to worry about. You'd best go on up to your room and finish your homework and then head into your bath. I think we'll order pizza in tonight. We can still get it from Mario's."

Angela didn't want Matthew hearing any more than he had to. She waited until he'd gone up the stairs, with only a short protest. She turned to her mother. "Can you ring through the pizza order Mum? Make it enough for everyone – Jimmy's staying too. The number's stuck to the fridge."

"I will, but shouldn't we ring the police first?"

"I think I need to speak to my Friday client before we do that. I need to find out what he's been up to. He might be able to tell us who those men were, and what the risks to us might be. I don't want to stir up more trouble than I need to."

Louise shook her head dubiously. "Well, you know what you're doing, I suppose. I'll organise that pizza—or three large perhaps?" she said, eyeing Jimmy's middle.

Angela led Jimmy into the front room where she could speak to him more privately. She wasn't quite ready to answer her mother's questions.

"Jimmy, we can't call the police. They'll start asking too many questions, like how do I know Stephen Lundy, for instance. I don't need them poking around in my life."

"There is that, Miss Angelique. I'll put the word out with my contacts and see if anyone knows anything."

"Good thinking." A look of disbelief crossed her face. "Jimmy—the black Volvo—you were right. It must have been staking *me* out. They know where I live; they must have followed us."

"I swear they didn't. I'm so careful —I was watching the traffic. They were here before us, so they already knew where you lived. I must be slipping in my old age." His face was flushed and brow furrowed. "If this is my fault, I'm so sorry, Miss Angelique. I was convinced we weren't followed."

As she looked unseeing from the front window, his words bounced around her head. Of course not. Why hadn't she realised? Pushing the hair from her face, she turned to face Jimmy, her voice tight and constrained.

"We might not have been followed at all. If we had been, they would have known I wasn't at home. I think they were given this address."

"What do you mean? Who by?"

"Mr Thursday. Last night he told me that he'd investigated my background. He knew about Matthew and probably knows where I live." She looked at Jimmy with dawning horror. "It sounds incredible but he must be behind this."

5 – A Breach in Security

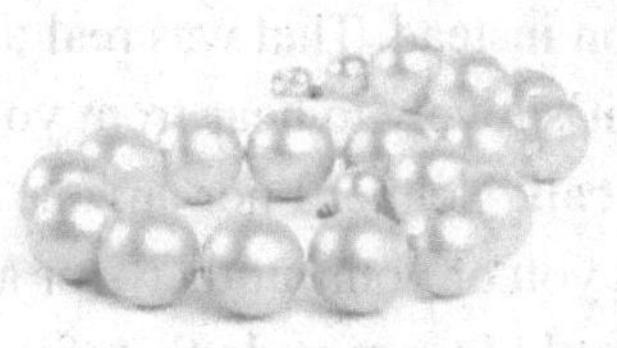

The more she thought about it, the more convinced she was it had to be him. Angela had retrieved the card for Luke Johnson from her handbag. Her fingers were shaking as she dialled the direct number. He picked up after a couple of seconds.

"You bastard! How dare you threaten my son! I don't know what your game is, but you won't succeed by intimidating me," she hissed.

"Angelique? Is that you? I've no idea what you're talking about."

Her voice rose a notch. The duplicity of the man made her all the angrier. Jimmy quickly moved to shut the door leading to the kitchen.

"You admitted you'd researched my background and knew about Matthew. Did you think I wouldn't put two and two together and realise you were behind this invasion? You've been conning me."

"Whoa! Just hold on a minute. Why don't you tell me what this is all about?"

"There's no need to pretend. You know exactly what's happened. Your thugs didn't find me —they threatened my mother and my son instead. That was real tough of them."

"Angelique, it's lovely to hear from you but this is a totally confusing call. Neither I nor anyone operating on my behalf has visited you or your mother—or anyone else to do with you. Why would I want to do that, for chrissake? Why don't you tell me what's happened?"

Angela's mind was racing. He sounded genuine. She desperately didn't want it to be him, but was he fooling her? If Luke Johnson wasn't behind the visit, who was? It didn't make sense. Her hand clutching the phone was clammy. The series of events was difficult to process. She glanced quickly at Jimmy, who was hovering within hearing range, shrugging her shoulders at him.

"I appear to have been under surveillance for a couple of days. Before I arrived home tonight, some thugs burst into my home and threatened my mother and my son."

"Were they hurt?"

"No, just shocked, I think."

"Give me your address. I'll come straight around."

"I thought you already knew everything about me. You must have my address already. Why should I let you anywhere near us?"

"Angelique—I don't get down to that level of detail and I don't retain information that isn't crucial. Once I re-assured

70

myself that you didn't have nefarious intentions, I moved on. Now do you want some help or not?"

She heard the door open behind her and Matthew entered the room, clad in his pyjamas. His face was flushed and glowing from his bath.

"Has the pizza man come yet, Mum? I'm starving."

At the sight of her young son, a wave of emotion swept over Angela. She couldn't take the risk of anything happening to him. At least he hadn't lost his appetite. She wasn't sure why, but she believed Luke Johnson when he said he wasn't involved. If that was the case, she needed all the support she could get. She needed to make sense of what had just happened.

Jimmy's eyebrows shot up as she dictated her address. She felt herself colouring and turned her back so as not to be distracted. She would explain to him when the call was finished.

"I'll be there shortly," Luke said. "I'll call you when I'm outside so you know it's okay to open the door."

"That shouldn't be necessary. Jimmy, my driver stayed with us and anyway, the pizza delivery man from Mario's will be here shortly."

"Just don't take any risks," he repeated and terminated the call.

Thirty minutes later footsteps were heard outside and the front doorbell rang.

"Yay—Pizza!" Matthew cried. "Did you order garlic bread as well?"

"You stay with your nan, Mattie," Jimmy said. "I'll open the door this time."

The pizza delivery man was on the doorstep. Jimmy checked the street behind him before ushering the man inside, quickly shutting the front door. Angela came forward with her purse to pay for the pizzas, and only then did the man take off his cap and jacket with upturned collar to reveal that it was Luke. Her heart picked up a pace.

"Luke! What are you doing with pizzas?"

"I said I was coming. I didn't want to rock up to the house and advertise my presence if you were still being watched. I dropped in at Mario's and picked up your order. He kindly lent me the clothing. We go back a bit. You'd better eat these while they're hot."

Matthew's eyes widened when he saw they had a visitor, even though it was one bearing food.

"It's okay Mattie—Luke's a friend."

Matthew appraised him silently, his eyes expressing the level of mistrust he clearly felt.

"Hi Mattie," said Luke. "I'm a friend of your mother's. Besides the pizzas, I brought some chicken wings and ribs as well. Smells good, doesn't it?"

He'd hit on the right strategy for building a young boy's trust. They all collected around the dining table.

"I hope you don't mind if I join you. I hadn't eaten when I received your call, and didn't want to delay getting here."

Angela found it unsettling to have Luke seated at her dining table. The subtle scent of aftershave she'd noticed the previous night was still present, and she had an almost irresistible urge to nuzzle up to him, inhaling it and him with it. She focussed on introductions instead.

"Thank you for coming. Mother, this is Luke Johnson. I met him one evening when Sasha had invited people over. He thought that he might be able to help us deal with this situation. Luke, this is my mother, Louise Benson."

He was the epitome of decorum, giving no indication on the nature of their relationship. He listened attentively while Louise recounted the events associated with the uninvited guests.

"And they want you to grant them access to who?"

Angela coloured again. She couldn't see any way around disclosing the identity of Mr Friday. It was a tricky situation.

"Stephen Lundy. I have an appointment with him on Friday. Whoever these people are, they've obviously done their homework on me and my movements. Jimmy has seen the car this week parked near my office."

"Stephen Lundy?" interrupted Louise, "but isn't he the son of that media baron? You don't mean him, surely?"

"Yes, I do. I do some contract work for him on Fridays—some of his bookkeeping."

"You never mentioned that you knew him." Louise was astonished.

"I don't talk about clients, Mum. I didn't think it was important. Anyway, I prefer to leave my work at work, if you know what I mean."

She sneaked a quick look at Luke. One eyebrow lifted sardonically, but he didn't pass any comment. There were other things on his mind.

"Well, this is Wednesday evening. That leaves Thursday to find out who or what's behind this. Have you notified Lundy?"

"Not yet. I'd better do that. It sounds so ludicrous I hardly know what to say to him."

"… and the next issue to address," Luke continued, "is your safety."

"We'll be fine," Angela replied. "Jimmy's checked out the security here."

Jimmy folded his arms and addressed his comments to Luke. "I've had a look around, and I wasn't impressed. Anyone with intent could gain entry; there's no clear view of the street; no security cameras; and no alternative exit. It's not safe at all."

"Jimmy! You didn't say anything about this earlier."

"I was assessing the lie of the land, and biding my time. My view is that you can't stay here."

"I agree," Luke said decisively. "You'll have to come and stay with me."

"I can't do that," Angela protested. "I have to look after Matthew and my mother."

"I meant all of you, of course. I didn't expect they would stay behind." He turned to the boy. "Matthew, your Nan has told me about your unwelcome visitors earlier today, so I'm suggesting you all stay with me for a few days while we sort this out. Is that okay with you?"

"I can look after my mum," the boy answered fiercely. "If those men come back here, I'll hide so they won't find me. If they try to touch my mum, I'll hit them."

"I wouldn't expect anything less, mate," Luke responded gravely. "I'll bet you'd put up a good fight. We're going to trick them though by not being here at all."

"I haven't agreed to this yet," Angela interjected. It was a crazy idea. Much as being close to Luke had tantalising possibilities, this was not how she had imagined doing it. "Matthew and I can stay with my mother for a few days."

"If you don't mind me sayin', Miss Angelique," said Jimmy, "I don't think that would be a good idea. If these people have been doing their homework, they'll know who Mrs B is and can easily find out where she lives."

"Well, they're probably watching the house now then," snapped Angela. "They'll have watched who arrived and they'll watch us leave. What's the point?" She fixed Luke with an unblinking stare.

"I've thought of that," said Jimmy, ignoring the frosty atmosphere. "Earlier I slipped out the back door and over the rear fence. Your neighbours never heard a thing. I came out onto the rear street and did a surreptitious tour of the block. There was nobody suspicious that I could see. They probably think you're so intimidated they don't have to stand guard tonight. They know where to find you anyway—or at least they think they do. It's a good idea if you clear out of here for a few days, and while you're gone, I'll arrange installation of monitored security, and a digital door viewer. Then you can see who's outside."

"That's settled," said Luke authoritatively. "If you pack up a few things, I'll bring the car to the front of the house. I left it parked around the corner."

"I'll take Mrs. B home to get her essentials," said Jimmy, "and then I can check out the security there as well. I'll make sure nobody's lying in wait and then I'll deliver her to your place, Mr Johnson."

"Thank you, Jimmy," said Louise. "I'll feel more secure knowing you're with me. I don't have to come to your home though," she said, addressing Luke. "If you're looking after my daughter and grandson, that should be enough. I'm sure these people have no real interest in me." She paused, clearly puzzled. "I still don't really understand though. Why are these people trying to get to Stephen Lundy through you?"

"I'm not sure," Angela replied slowly. "When I meet with him, he doesn't have any security support. Perhaps they think he's more vulnerable at this time."

In her mind, she pictured the man in his usual state on Fridays—buck naked and unconcerned about the affairs of the world. She suppressed the smile threatening to break out at the thought. She studiously did not make eye contact with Luke.

"C'mon Mattie—we'd better get your clothes and anything you'll need for school tomorrow. I'll pack an overnight bag too. Luke, perhaps you can give Jimmy your address and contact details. I'm assuming he hasn't collated this information in any research he might have done on my behalf."

The look she gave Luke spoke volumes.

Interesting. Angelique had set the dog on me before, or at least she inferred that she had. Luke laughed to himself. The situation in which she found herself was not funny, but she hadn't lost her spirit.

While she packed for herself and Mattie, he waited in the lounge room. The furnishings were tasteful, but he wouldn't have expected anything less.

He wondered over to the bookshelf, curious to see what she might read. The collection ranged from women's fiction, through to some literary fiction. There were quite a few books on financial analysis and investments strategies. *Why am I not surprised?* A few framed photos sat on the shelves as well, along with odd items, like a seashell and a couple of vases. There were the inevitable photos of Angelique nursing Mattie as a baby, and others featuring Louise and Mattie.

None of the photos depicted a man, either with Angelique or Mattie. That was reassuring. There was nothing though that explained her background, why there wasn't a partner on the scene and why she was doing the work she was, except of course it was lucrative.

He heard footsteps moving overhead and then her voice drifting down from upstairs. "Got everything Mattie? We might not be back here for a couple of days. Come on—we can't keep Luke waiting."

Luke. At least she'd called him Luke. Already his mind was moving ahead to both the opportunities and consequences of having her under his roof. That was not to underestimate the danger she might be in. The invasion was a concern, but once that was dealt with, he would see if their relationship could be moved to a different level. Mattie was a cute kid. He wouldn't mind having a child around the place again.

He placed a call to his housekeeper. "Hi Maria—sorry about the late notice, but we'll be having some house-guests for a few days. I'm not sure how long. We'll need three of the bedrooms made up, one for a child. He could go into Peter's room."

"No problem, Mr Luke. When will they arrive?"

"In about half an hour."

"Oh, my lord. I'd better get moving. The beds are all made up, but I'll need to check the bathrooms and a few other things. The kettle will be on when you get here."

Luke smiled to himself. He knew Maria would relish having the visitors in the house, and others beside himself to appreciate her cooking. She wasn't the only one full of anticipation.

While packing, Angela took advantage of the moment of privacy to use her work phone to quickly call Stephen Lundy.

"Stephen? It's Angelique."

"Angelique? What a surprise! One moment; I'll move to a quieter room." There was a pause before he spoke again. "Have you decided to take me up on my offer after all? The apartment in Sydney's still available. Name the day."

"Unfortunately, the reason for my call is not so pleasant. Have you upset anyone lately? Owe anyone money? Neglected any obligations?"

"Is this some sort of riddle? I'm confused."

"I'm confused too. This evening, two men forced their way into my home looking for me. I wasn't here, so they threatened my family instead. It seems they've had me under surveillance for a while."

"What's that to do with me?"

"They know you regularly visit me on Friday. They instructed my mother, emphatically you understand, that unless I provide them with access to you presumably this Friday, they will target my son."

There was a silence on the other end of the phone.

"Stephen? Are you still there?"

"Yes… yes… I'm trying to make sense of it all. Who were these people?"

"I've no idea, but they weren't very friendly. I'm about to quit my home for a few days, staying in a secret location with my family. I suggest you take precautions as well. Oh, and I think we might cancel your Friday appointment."

Her whimsical tone did not portray her inner turmoil. Angelique was always in control, and she was not about to indicate anything else.

"But, do you really think… I mean what if…?" Stephen trailed off into confusion.

"I've got to go now. I'll call you tomorrow," she said, and disconnected the call.

More than an hour later, they were assembled in Luke's palatial home. It was nestled on the slopes of foothills overlooking the city, with many of the rooms benefitting from stunning views of the skyline by day and the city lights by night. His housekeeper greeted them at the door and showed the guests to their rooms. Maria welcomed them warmly. She queried what needs they might have and showed them the essential rooms in the house—the perfect host.

"Thank goodness there's a sensible woman in the house," Louise whispered to Angela. "I don't know what to think of all this, I really don't."

"Don't worry Mum; it won't be for long. I'm sorry you've been dragged into this mess. As soon as we've sorted out what's happening. we can each go back to our own homes."

Matthew was allocated a room which was intended for a young child, judging by the books on the shelves and the posters on the walls. It occurred to Angela that there was a lot she didn't know about Luke Johnson. She didn't think he was married, but there was evidently a child in his life. She'd done more research into his business than into the man. The housekeeper brought up a warm mug of milk and Angela put her son to bed before joining the others downstairs in the lounge room.

"Matthew's all settled?"

Luke had been in deep discussion with Jimmy, but the men stopped talking when she entered the room.

"Yes, he's fine and Mum's gone to bed. So tell me— what have you two been discussing?"

The two men exchanged a glance. Jimmy cleared his throat before speaking.

"It's obvious you can't go back to the harbour-side apartment until this blows over. You'll need to stay here until we find out what's behind all of this."

"So you've both been deciding what is and isn't safe for me to do? I can make my own decisions, in case you both need reminding. As it happens, I'll need to pick up some papers from my office tomorrow, but I rang Stephen Lundy to outline events for him and as for tomorrow," she fixed Luke with a meaningful stare, "I don't think I need to linger at the apartment."

"Can I get them for you, Miss Angelique? Then you won't have to go out."

"And who's looking out for you Jimmy? No, I can get them myself, but I would like you to come with me. Perhaps we can use a different car tomorrow?"

"That's not a problem," interjected Luke. "You can use one of mine. This is all very reactive though. We need to be putting together a plan of action. Before we do that, what can I fetch you to drink? I think a Scotch might be in order."

"A man after my own heart," declared Jimmy.

While Luke busied himself with preparing the drinks, Angela took a moment to look around her. You could learn a lot about a person from their home. There weren't any photos on display which might have indicated who else was in his life. The room was expansive and tastefully furnished, but not with a feminine touch. She guessed it was the work of a designer, rather than indicative of Luke's creativity. As far as she could tell, the housekeeper was the only other person living there, well except for the mystery child. What was his or her relationship to Luke?

Luke handed her the brandy she had requested, his fingers grazing hers. She didn't dare look at him in case he saw what just his touch could do to her. If he ignited that fire, how would she put it out?

"Did Stephen Lundy give you any idea what this was all about?"

"I don't think he knew. He sounded just as confused as I was."

"Well we've got to find out or you'll be looking over your shoulder forever, to say nothing of worrying about Matthew's safety. There's also police involvement to consider. We need to get Lundy here as part of any discussions—unless you want to comply with the demands of course."

Angela delivered the look of scorn the comment deserved.

"It's too late tonight, but we should meet with Stephen tomorrow. He'll have arranged his own security by now so that much is taken care of. We can't stay here forever though so finding out who these people are and putting a stop to their shenanigans needs to happen quickly."

She licked her lips pensively, savouring the brandy. There was a sweet after taste, complimenting the heat in her belly. Her lips tingled, and for a fleeting moment she thought of what it would be like to give Luke a brandy-flavoured kiss, before making herself focus on the discussion.

"I should let Sasha know too. She and Renato usually have an ear to the ground. There's very little that goes on in this city they don't get to know about."

"I've already put feelers out through my networks," Jimmy said. "The boys will tell me if there's anyone on their radar."

"There's probably not much else we can do tonight," Luke said. "The main thing is to ensure that you, your mother and Matthew are safe. We can re-group tomorrow and discuss our strategy. If you can invite Lundy here, that would be helpful."

Tossing down the last of his drink, Jimmy stood up. "On that note, I'll take my leave. What time should I pick you up, Miss Angelique?"

"I might go early if it's okay with you. I normally leave home after Matthew has gone to school so if anyone is familiar with my usual pattern and watching out for me, they'll expect me to do the same. Can you pick me up at 7:30?"

"Park around the back, Jimmy," instructed Luke, "then you can swap your car for another in the garage. Take your pick. The housekeeper will have the keys."

"I'll take the one with the darkest windows. See you in the morning."

"Drive safe Jimmy," Angela called. "Check for any strange vehicles on your way home."

Only last night this woman was tantalising me, and here she is in my home. Life is full of little surprises. "So, Angelique—or should I be calling you Angela? That just leaves us," Luke said, eyeing her over the rim of his glass.

She stared at him defiantly.

"Your choice. In front of Mattie and my mother, Angela is better. It's less confusing for them."

There was a moment's silence. When she did speak again, she sounded stilted.

"Thank you for putting us up tonight. I didn't mean to put you to this level of inconvenience. I'm sorry for accusing you of being responsible. I'll arrange a meeting with Stephen tomorrow and hopefully this will be soon sorted, and we'll be out of your hair."

"That's assuming I want you out of my hair. Having you close by could have certain benefits."

Her eyes widened slightly at those words.

"I admit though," he continued, "if I'd ever fantasised about varying my arrangement with you, it had not encompassed a group deal involving your mother and your son as well."

She lifted her head a fraction. "You're not responsible for us. I can take care of my family. I've been doing it for years."

"...and with remarkable panache and creativity. Is it an option that Mattie can stay with his father until all the drama is over? I don't suppose he's in any way behind all of this in some warped attempt to get his hands on Mattie?"

"If that man wants to see Mattie, all he has to do is ask, but there's not much risk of it happening. He's never shown any interest and I doubt he'd come anywhere near us. He'd be too scared I'd hit him up for child support." Her scorn was palpable. "He needn't worry because I don't want anything from him and that wouldn't explain the involvement of Stephen Lundy."

"Speaking of Lundy, I assume he's also engaged your executive coaching services?"

"I'm not at liberty to discuss my professional relationship with Stephen. If it's alright with you, I think it's time I retired for the night."

It was a not-so-subtle change of subject. Luke didn't like being played for a fool. "Are you running away? Is that how you end awkward conversations?"

A look of annoyance skittered across her face. Clearly, she wasn't going to discuss that aspect of her life. An inner voice chided him. *Don't push things Luke. You might not like the answer, and this is not the time. Play your cards carefully.*

"Not at all. There's nothing to talk about. It's been an eventful day and emotionally a bit stressful, that's all."

"I'm not surprised." Luke drained the rest of his scotch. Closing the gap between them, he removed the glass she was still holding from her grasp, and placed it on the side table. In a decisive movement, he pulled her to him.

"When we're in your apartment, you make all the rules. You're one tough, uncompromising woman. Now we're in my territory and I have a few rules of my own, the first being that when in private, I'm entitled to a goodnight kiss."

He didn't give her time to digest that remark before making good on his first rule. She didn't respond initially, but he felt her melt against him. He was aroused by the sensation of her body pressed against his. The kiss was tender, promising, tantalising even. Then he pushed her from him, holding her at arm's length.

"Rule number two is that I don't make assumptions. Good night, Angelique. Sleep tight."

When Luke released her, Angela lurched momentarily before regaining her balance and her composure. With only a momentary look into the eyes that still threatened to devour her, she turned and fled to the room she'd been given. His words made her understand what had been making her uncomfortable – the change in power dynamics. The sooner she was back in her own home, the better. The man could stir the heat in her more than any other.

She sat on the edge of her bed, collecting her thoughts. What did Luke think of her, now he'd learned more of her background? Their professional relationship could never be the same, of that much she was sure.

Rousing herself, she slipped into the adjoining room and checked on her son. He was fast asleep, the book he'd evidently been reading fallen to the floor by the bed. He was splayed out in the sleep of the innocent, and Angela was glad the stresses of earlier events hadn't prevented him from dropping off. Leaving a light kiss on his forehead, she crept out of the room, shutting the door quietly behind her.

There was an ensuite bathroom attached to her bedroom. She quickly showered and after pulling a cotton nightgown over her head, climbed into bed.

She was still far from sleep, when her bedroom door quietly opened, and Luke slipped into the room. She sat up, startled by the intrusion. In the dim light, she could see he was dressed in a bathrobe, and possibly, only that.

"I didn't get around to telling you rule number three. When Thursday afternoon commitments are disrupted, that means they can be transferred to Wednesday nights."

Shucking off the robe and slipping beneath the covers, he slipped into bed beside her.

"Of course," he murmured huskily, "you can always invoke rule number two if you want."

In answer, she slipped off her nightgown and reached for him.

6 – Making Sense of it All

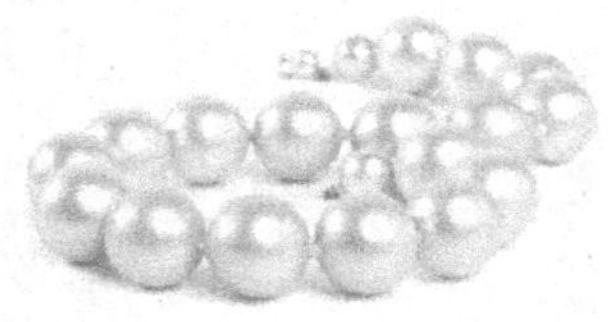

When Angela awoke, she was alone, and for that she was grateful. She didn't want awkward questions from Matthew, or her mother for that matter. There was a dent in the pillow to indicate Luke had spent the night beside her. She rolled towards it and found it still carried the faint scent of his aftershave. The memory of the nocturnal events came flooding back. It was a long time since she had shared her bed with anyone other than Matthew. What had she been thinking when allowing him to stay? He was a client! What if Matthew had come looking for her? Her head told her this was not going to end well, but it was not her head guiding her actions the night before.

Resolving to think about it when she had more time, she pushed herself out of bed and into the shower. She had an early start and needed to be ready before Jimmy arrived.

Peeking in Matthew's room, she found him out of bed and playing with a box of Lego.

"See what I made, Mum? This room's got some cool stuff in it."

"I can see that. Just remember that it belongs to someone else. Be sure to put everything back where you found it."

"Who does it belong to?"

"I've no idea." *I don't feel comfortable asking either but now I'm really curious.* "C'mon; we'll see what we can find in the kitchen for breakfast."

The house was quiet as they made their way downstairs, but the housekeeper and Louise were in deep discussion in the kitchen. They were clutching coffee mugs and the aroma of freshly percolated coffee filled the room.

"You two are up early," Angela remarked. "Can I find a bit of toast or something for Matthew?"

Maria jumped off her stool. "We can certainly do better than a piece of toast. Would you like cereal, eggs, fruit, pancakes… We can organise anything."

The small boy's eyes widened. "Can I have pancakes?"

"Sure, you can. And for you?" she asked of Angela. "Would you like to start with a cup of coffee, or perhaps tea?"

I must have died and gone to heaven, thought Angela. Fancy having a housekeeper who makes your breakfast and organises everything for you.

"Just coffee and a slice of toast will be fine. I can make it myself if you point me in the right direction." She turned to her mother. "Mum, I don't think Matthew should go to school today. Until we find out what's going on, this might be the safest place for you both. Are you able to stay here with him?" She dropped a slice of bread into the toaster and took the mug of coffee Maria had poured.

"Of course, sweetheart," her mother responded, "but you're not going out are you? Do you think that's wise? Surely the accounting can wait for a day or so?"

She didn't trust herself to look at her mother. She could never let her know exactly what her figure-work entailed.

"I won't be alone. Jimmy will escort me to the office where I need to collect some papers. I won't stay there for long. I need to make some phone calls and decide on our plan of action. We can't stay here forever."

"Mum, I like it here."

"I'm sure you do Matthew, but we've got our own house to live in. We'll be back there very soon. I want you to stay inside today. I'll ring your school and tell them not to expect you. Be sure to do what your Nan tells you, and if there are any problems, you can call me. Okay?" The toaster popped and she retrieved her slice of toast.

There was a knock at the back door and Maria opened it to reveal Jimmy on the doorstep.

"Morning all. No problems in the middle of the night? Are you ready to go, Miss Angelique?"

Before she had a chance to respond, Luke came into the kitchen as well. His eyes met Angela's briefly and she coloured, remembering the night before. She felt a tingling in her breasts, her nipples hardening of their own accord. The intensity of the sensation made her inwardly gasp. She looked away, lest he read what was going through her mind. His proposal to them all surprised her.

90

"Jimmy, I'll drive Angela today. It might be advisable if you stayed here and ensured the household was safe."

Jimmy looked towards Angela, eyebrows raised. She shrugged and nodded. He turned back to Luke. "If you say so, Luke. No-one will come to any danger while I'm here." His shoulders slumped slightly and his disappointment was tangible.

Angela knew he had been looking forward to driving one of the cars from Luke's garage. She was reassured in knowing he would be staying with Matthew and her mother. Her feelings about Luke accompanying her were a different matter. "Look, you don't need to drive me around. I'm sure you have your own business matters to attend to. Your life and work doesn't stop just because I have a drama to deal with."

"I'll decide about my business operations, and as far as driving you around—it makes sense. If anyone is trailing you today, they won't be looking for my car or me. If you're wanting to get your business done early, we'd better leave now. While you're attending to whatever admin issues and executive coach has, I can do some of of my own, if you have a small corner in which I can work."

Angela didn't have cause to object, other than the fact that the apartment was her own private sanctum. Sure, she entertained the clients there, but they only saw as much as she allowed. No-one entered her office. She paused for a beat, conscious of the faces looking at her. She would have to manage the issue as best she could.

"You're probably right. Give me time to finish my toast and I'll get my briefcase."

The Audi A4 Sedan was already out of the garage and waiting in the driveway. Angela opened the back door, intending to get in until Luke intervened.

"I think you should ride in the front. It won't look like you're arriving in a chauffeured limo then and they might be watching out for that if it's how you usually arrive. I chose this vehicle because it has the darkest windows. It also has a bit of power if we need it."

"Are you directing all aspects of my life now?" She was feeling uncharacteristically churlish. She knew it was petty but felt like getting in the back seat anyway. With compressed lips, she slid into the front passenger seat and fastened the seat belt.

"Would you rather I left you, Matthew and your mother to the mercy of these people?"

She took a deep breath and then exhaled slowly. He had no right to bring Mattie and her mother into this conversation. "No, of course not. I'm sorry—I'm not used to someone else making decisions on my behalf. Perhaps you could discuss things with me first."

Luke didn't respond immediately. He flicked a quick glance at her as he pulled out of the driveway, after checking the street for unknown vehicles.

"I'm not meaning to take over. I guess I'm used to making quick decisions. I don't usually have the time or the need to discuss them with anyone else. I'll try to remember."

The next five minutes was passed in silence, until he spoke again.

"So—what's your plan of action? Tell me how you're proposing to deal with this threat to Matthew and yourself."

Angela had been turning this question over and outlined the issues as she saw them.

"Don't forget it's first and foremost a threat to Stephen Lundy. Matthew is being used as a lever to force me to comply with their demands. Keeping Matthew out of their clutches is my first priority but it's a short-term solution. I'm not keen on buying into Stephen's problems, whatever they may be, but don't want to be responsible for him coming to harm either."

She glanced sideways to judge Luke's response. They were almost shoulder-touching distance, and she was acutely aware of the proximity. He was focussed on his driving, giving her the opportunity to observe his profile. The small frown of concentration indicated he was listening to what she was saying.

She continued. "When I'm at my desk, I'll call Sasha first to keep her informed and also see if she or Renato have any idea who might be behind this. Together, they know many of the movers and shakers around town, and there is not much that slips past them. Then I'll call Stephen and set up a time for him to meet with us—at your place, if that's okay with you. By then, he'll have had time to do his own investigations, and hopefully will have something to tell us with a proposal of how he's going to deal with it."

Privately, she was wondering what to do about next week's clients —Mr Monday, Mr Tuesday and Mr Wednesday. Hopefully there would be no need to tell them anything and their appointments would continue without complication. She shuddered thinking how Mr Tuesday would react. Her business would disintegrate in a flash and she wanted to have her alternative plans in place before that happened. That was one conundrum she wasn't about to reveal to Luke. Added to that was ambiguity about her current relationship with him, and what was going to happen about the Thursday time slot.

Luke had calls of his own to make.

"While you attend to your affairs, I'll make some enquiries as well. I'll follow up discreetly with some of my contacts and see if anyone is aware of reasons why Lundy might be targeted. Is there anyone he's offended that he shouldn't have, that sort of thing."

He pulled into the basement carpark when the security grill opened and halted by the elevator door.

"I'll let you out here, then do a quick tour of surrounding streets to see if I can spot this Volvo you've described, or anything else that presses the alert button, then I'll be back. I'll wait until you're in the elevator. Call me when you're safely in the apartment."

"I doubt there'll be any problem," she replied. "After all, it's a secure car park but checking the adjoining streets is a good idea. I'll see you soon. I'll even put the kettle on."

"Stay safe, Angelique."

The look he gave her was enigmatic. With a quick smile she slipped out of the car and pressed the button for the elevator. As the doors closed behind her, she saw that as promised, Luke was still waiting in full view. It was always possible someone could access the elevator at ground or one of the other levels, but they didn't, and she made a quick call to Luke as requested when she was safely inside the apartment.

It seemed incredible, but Luke was behaving as though he genuinely cared for her. Angela savoured the feeling, allowing herself a hint of a smile. She couldn't remember when she'd last basked in the warmth of that feeling, if she ever had. Where could it lead though? Nowhere, and that thought was just as devastating as the knowledge of the threats against her son.

The adrenaline surge heightened his sense of vigilance. These men could be armed. He could look after himself; at least he hoped he could. This was outside the area of his usual expertise. He'd never forgive himself if anything happened to Angelique, or Angela, whatever he should call her. From what he'd learned of her so far, it wouldn't surprise him if she held a black belt in some form of martial art, but even so, they still had no idea who they were dealing with.

Jimmy's expertise and his contacts meant they held a few cards in their hands and hopefully the element of surprise would do the rest. Angela was fortunate to have him working for her. Luke wondered about the man's background. It would make interesting listening, once this immediate drama was over. He was a useful person to have onside.

There was nothing untoward he could see in the streets, certainly no black Volvos. He tried not to be too obvious as he peered at parked vehicles as he cruised past.

His thoughts turned to what might happen when this episode was over. Things would never be the same again between he and Angelique. The weekly commitment would be forever changed. The understanding on which the arrangement was based had crumbled in the last thirty-six hours, but what would replace it? He had no way of answering that question.

Her first task was to check the apartment for anything that shouldn't be on view, but she was worrying needlessly. She always tidied fastidiously before leaving each afternoon. Luke could set up on the dining table while she was making her calls in the office. Second task was to fill the kettle and organise the tea things. She knew Luke's preferences.

Taking advantage of the private moment before he arrived, Angela placed her call to Sasha. "Thank you for a lovely evening. You have a talent for inviting the right combination of people. Tanya McNeil was an inspired choice."

"She was," the older woman responded dryly, "but I'm not sure how much you and Luke Johnson heard from outside."

"It was easier to hear ourselves talk, but we could still listen to Tanya's recital. It was beautiful." It was time to change the subject away from Luke. "I need to ask you something."

Sasha was quick to sense the change in vibe. "What is it? What's happened?"

"Sasha, something unbelievable. I've been threatened. Someone wants me to give them access to Stephen Lundy this Friday, and if I don't they say they'll seize Matthew to force my hand."

"That's a ridiculous threat. Who's behind this?" The older woman sounded incredulous.

"I've absolutely no idea. I wasn't at home when they paid a call on Matthew and my mother last night. I was wondering if you'd heard any scuttle-butt. Do you know if Stephen Lundy has trodden on any powerful toes, or does he have debts he hasn't paid—anything like that?"

"I wouldn't have thought there were any skeletons of that nature in the closet. The family have always been known for their philanthropic works, especially his mother, and his father has never let Stephen forget he comes from a privileged position. He was not allowed to be a spoilt brat. I don't know why anyone would have it in for that young man. The family are filthy rich of course; there's always that."

"Without ruffling feathers, could you make some enquiries?" Angela asked.

"Of course, my dear. In the meantime, what are you doing about *your* safety?"

"I can't talk for long, because he'll be here in a minute, but last night we all stayed with Luke Johnson. Matthew and my mother are still at his home, and Jimmy is standing guard. Luke accompanied me to the apartment today. I wanted to collect some papers and make a couple of calls."

"That's an unexpected arrangement," Sasha commented. "Please don't take any risks. I'd be devastated if anything happened to you. You know how fond I am of you and I speak for Renato as well."

"And I'm very fond of you too. You have both done so much for me. This whole incident has the potential to derail my current business though—it's obviously tricky where Luke Johnson is concerned—so there's even more pressure on me to look at new business ventures."

"How was your salon visit yesterday?"

"Really helpful. I'm supposed to be catching up with Wendy tomorrow morning. It's given me a lot to consider; I haven't had time to think about it in depth."

"Understandably. Stay safe all of you."

As she disconnected the call, Luke buzzed from below, requesting access and she pressed the release button allowing him into the elevator. She still didn't open the door to the apartment before checking through the peephole that he was alone.

"Why do I get the feeling that you're overdressed?" he said as she let him in. "It's Thursday—shouldn't my welcome be a little different?"

"You said you were going to make some calls" Angela replied tartly. "I wouldn't want to distract you."

He sighed theatrically. "It's going to take me a while to get used to Angela in the place of Angelique. I'm not sure how I'll cope."

"I can always offer you a cold shower if that will help, but I was about to flick the switch on the kettle in the kitchen."

He followed her to the kitchen, seizing her from behind and nuzzling the back of her neck. "I think I'd rather flick your switch, but I can see it will have to wait."

She swivelled around in his grasp so that she was facing him, her body pressed against his. She was aware of his instant response, and caught her breath in the effort to hide hers. She slipped her hand inside the open neck of his shirt, relishing the sensation of his bare skin. Reaching up, she kissed him softly, tantalisingly. "For now, it will have to be a rain check."

He groaned and pushed her away. "Unhand me, woman, and make that cup of tea before I have to take the shower option."

She laughed and released him, thinking that it was probably she who needed the cold shower. She couldn't let him know that. Theirs was a commercial relationship and she had to keep that in mind. It was pointless to let her emotions run away with her.

"I've spoken to Sasha. She and Renato are putting out feelers to see what they can discover about the Lundys as well. The dining table is free for you to work. There is a power point on the wall if you need it." Maintaining a business-like demeanour was her best defence against her inner emotions.

Luke took his cue from her. "Thanks. If Lundy can join us at my home, we can discuss tactics with everyone present. I'll make calls to my network. Let me know when you're ready to go. I'll drop you back home and then do a couple of my own errands. "

Luke adjourned to the dining table and Angela returned to her office. She wasn't in the mood for sitting. Picking up her phone, she wandered over to the window. The scene on the harbour below, was just as she expected—serene, and ordered—just as her life had been the last time she looked at the view. What a difference a day could make.

She got through to Stephen. He still had no idea who or what was behind the threats, nor did his father, whom he'd consulted confidentially. In their line of business, with media ownership and interests in many diverse entities, they'd probably offended everyone in positions of power and influence at some time, but none specifically came to mind. None that would resort to this degree of retribution. He'd organised personal security though and agreed to meet with her late afternoon. In the meantime, he would keep making his own enquiries.

Angela attended to a few trade transactions and updated her records. Now wasn't the time to continue her studies. She packed some of the files she needed in her brief case and shut down her computer. It was time to go back to Luke's place.

~

Louise promised to occupy Mattie while the discussions took place, and Angela preferred that neither of them were visible. Her privacy had been compromised enough already. When Stephen arrived, he was without his usual suave confidence. He was escorted to the door by a man with a square head and buzz cut, who retreated to the car once Stephen advised him it was safe to do so. He looked as though he hadn't slept well, and glanced quickly behind him before entering the house. Once inside, he kept his back to the wall, casting uncertain looks towards Jimmy.

"I'm so sorry you've been dragged into this, Angelique. It's fortunate Luke here has been able to offer you sanctuary."

100

The two men exchanged appraising glances, and politely shook hands. Angela groaned inwardly. If Luke hadn't already guessed about Stephen, the use of the name Angelique would have confirmed it. There wasn't much she could do about that. Jimmy had joined them, and the four of them sat around the dining table, disclosing what they knew, which wasn't very much.

"I've honestly no idea who could be behind this," Stephen offered. "My life's an open book—well in areas that matter," he said, glancing at Angela with a hint of a smile. "There are lots of toes we've trodden on through the papers of course, but no one who's likely to come gunning for us. Anyway, control of that side of things rests more with my father."

"So what *do* you control?" Luke posed the question.

Stephen sat for a moment while he considered his answer. The distant chatter of voices in the kitchen filled the void.

"I focus on the overseas operations, principally with resort and casino development. If there was something happening in Australia, I'd wonder about a nimby protest, but even so I wouldn't expect it to be so extreme."

"What about the Asian connection?" Jimmy asked. "Don't you have a big deal in progress with one of our major Asian neighbours?"

"Yes, but there's no trouble that I know of. Were these men Asian?"

"No. That's about all we can say with confidence, so it's unlikely to be an Asian instigator. They tend to only trust their own when there's any muscle required. At least that's one avenue we can rule out," Jimmy asserted.

"There's just a faint possibility that occurs to me," said Stephen slowly.

Three sets of eyes swivelled in his direction, watching the frown of concentration on his face. In the ensuing silence, the muted voices in the kitchen, reminded Angela what was at stake here, or rather who. This wasn't just about Stephen.

"Don't leave us in suspense," demanded Luke.

"It was the Asian connection that reminded me. When I submitted my bid for this latest project, I was up against a Russian consortium. Those guys have some serious money and were confident the deal was theirs, but I did some careful relationship building. I won the contract and they were not happy about that."

Jimmy looked sceptical. "Does that mean you greased a few palms? No wonder they're upset."

Stephen threw a look of scorn in Jimmy's direction, but as Angela noticed, he didn't answer the question.

"Surely they wouldn't have followed you back to Australia? Wouldn't they just move on to the next project or find a new location if they've got that much money?"

"It can be a matter of pride with the Russians. They don't take kindly to losing; not this lot anyway. There were some veiled comments, but I didn't take any of it seriously. I'd forgotten about it until now."

"We'll that's fine," Angela interjected, "but what are we going to do? Do I have to remind you all that tomorrow is Friday? The Russian mafia is going to turn up at my apartment, and if Stephen isn't there and available, they're going to come looking for my son! We need a plan, because I am not putting Mattie in danger." She leaned forward, both hands on the table in front of her. There was silence as the three men absorbed her words.

Luke cleared his throat. "We'll have to lay a trap. You'll go to the apartment as usual, and when the men turn up, we'll nab them."

"You and whose army?" Angela demanded. "These men will probably be armed; have you thought about that? We don't know how many there'll be, and they'll overpower us and take Stephen anyway and if they don't, they'll come looking for Matthew."

Jimmy laid a protective hand on her arm. "Miss Angelique, I'm not going to let any of that happen. Nobody is going to hurt you or your son. I know I failed you in not intercepting that car, but it won't happen again. As soon as we sort out what's happening, I'll get a team of mates on the job. They've got the experience to handle this sort of thing."

Stephen leant forward. "I want to make it clear I'll bankroll any expenses. If other people are brought in, they'll be paid. It has to be on a confidential basis though. They can't talk about it."

"Let's consider the options logically." Luke had been leaning back in his chair, but now sat forward and looked at the others. "The first option of course is telling the police."

"No. No publicity." Stephen was emphatic

"I don't think that's a good idea." Angela shook her head decisively.

"Let's keep the police out of this if we can." said Jimmy.

"That sounds unanimous," he said. "I assume you all have sound reasons for that decision, but surely Stephen, you can control what gets into the papers?"

"Are you kidding? Something like this, the media would be all over it, even the divisions the family owns. It would have front page coverage, and would kill my current negotiations stone dead."

"Well, we can't have that," Luke said smoothly. "Not good for the bottom line at all."

Stephen glared. "I don't think you quite understand."

"No, I probably don't but we need to move on to option two."

"Which is?" Angela asked.

"We ignore them, stay away from the apartment, and hope they'll go away."

"That's not practical, is it? They'll come after Matthew and myself. We might be safe for now, but we can't stay here forever. It's not a viable option either."

"No, I didn't really think so," he agreed "but the 'do nothing' option still needed to be considered."

Jimmy's folded arms indicated his opinion, and Stephen just snorted, before getting up and starting to pace. "So what are you proposing?" he asked. "I assume you've got a suggestion up your sleeve?"

Angela chewed her lip as she sensed the vibe in the air. It wasn't going to help the situation if any antagonism were to develop. "Tell us what you're thinking."

Luke looked at her. "You go to the apartment as usual on Friday, with Jimmy driving you. It has to appear that everything is normal. Shortly before his appointment with you, Lundy drives to your apartment and follows his normal arrival routine. We'll have a retinue of people scattered around the place – picking up rubbish on the beach, painting the house across the road, riding a postal bike with a bag of letters; they'll all have a legitimate reason for doing what they're doing."

"So I go in like a sacrificial lamb. Then what? I just let them take me? I don't call that a plan. That's what we're trying to avoid." Stephen sounded unimpressed.

They all looked at Luke, who remained silent for a moment before exhaling heavily. "No, they won't take you because it won't actually be you in the car. We're approximately the same colouring and height. I'll drive your car in and perhaps wear your sunglasses, and do a basic makeover. I should look sufficiently like you to lure these people out into the open."

"So they take you instead," spluttered Angela. "Where's the sense in that?"

Even Jimmy looked confused.

"I would have thought that was obvious. We don't put Lundy at risk, but lure these men into the open. I had a word to the Building Manager today, and have arranged to get control of the elevator as well, just for a brief period. His son is going to start a period of work experience with Johnson Hydrology. Angelique will let them into the carpark, and that will remove them from the street and public view. No matter what button they press in the elevator, it won't take them out of the basement. A team will be waiting for them. They'll never make it up to the apartment and Angelique will not be put in danger."

He turned to address her. "All you have to do is take their call, and tell them to 'Come on up'. Don't leave the apartment until you're given the all clear. Don't let anyone other than Jimmy or myself into the apartment."

"Do you really think they'll fall for this?" she asked. "It seems almost too easy."

"My gut tells me this isn't a terribly sophisticated operation. It reeks of desperation rather than strategic planning."

"And what will you do with these men, once you've intercepted them?"

"You don't need to worry about that, Miss Angelique." Jimmy was emphatic. "Some subtle pressure will soon reveal who's behind all of it. What happens to them depends on how helpful they are. Then we go after the bloke."

"What if there's a woman behind it?" Angela asked.

Stephen had been quiet through this exchange but now looked incredulous. "No woman could possibly be responsible for this. There aren't any women in my life bearing me malice."

Angela smiled at him, deliberately avoiding Luke's eyes. "I'm sure there aren't, Stephen. That doesn't fit with my understanding of you at all." *You've always been such a pussy cat. Just don't explain to Luke how that understanding has come about.*

Luke's response was brusque. "I prefer to keep an open mind on this. Lundy, you'll need to be here early in the morning to give me your car. Jimmy and Angelique should take their usual car, and travel at the usual time for a Friday."

"I'm not going to sit here while everyone else is in the firing line. I want to be in on the action as well. After all, it's me they're looking for. I want to find out what this is all about."

Jimmy jumped in with a suggestion. "I'll set you up as one of the house painters. You'll have to keep a cap on and wear a pair of overalls. Most importantly you can't let them eyeball you until after we nab them. You'll put the whole operation in jeopardy. You have to follow directions implicitly. If you don't, you might endanger others—Miss Angelique, for instance."

"I'll do whatever you suggest—I just can't hide behind you."

Angela saw Luke roll his eyes, but he didn't comment. Her thoughts flicked to what she had to do in the morning and she suddenly remembered she was supposed to accompany the operations manager on more salon visits. She'd better cancel. She would ring her after current arrangements were finalised.

Jimmy jumped up to make some phone calls, and to marshal his team. For the umpteenth time, Angela was glad Jimmy was in her life. She felt much safer knowing he was looking out for her and Matthew. Luke and Stephen made their own arrangements. Leaving them to it, she made her way into the kitchen. It was time to ask Maria to put the kettle on.

When she looked around, Luke was there, leaning against the benchtop and watching her.

"If you feel this is too much, you can back out," he said. "I don't want to put you in danger."

"Backing out is not an option. There's too much at stake—like Matthew for instance."

With a nodded response, he turned to go back to the others.

"Why are you doing this?" Angela called after him. "Why are you helping Stephen?"

He looked at her for a moment, then reached out, sliding one finger down the side of her face. It was a soft touch, yet at the same time tantalizing. She caught her breath, and could feel her nipples tingling in response.

"Not here," she whispered. "Not here."

When he spoke, his voice was ragged. "Lundy is fortunate. Helping him is a result of helping you."

After Lundy left, Luke sought refuge in his bathroom and rinsed his face in cold water. It wasn't quite the same as a cold shower, but would have to do. Just touching the woman was enough to set off a tantilising response. He didn't want to rush her when her mind was so obviously on other things.

She'd asked a fair question. If he were honest with both himself and with Angela, he didn't care what strife Stephen Lundy got himself into. They knew each other socially, but before this had not had much to do with each other. Now that Luke had made his closer acquaintance, he was less than impressed. The man appeared to be petulant and a bit wet. What had Angela ever seen in him?

The threat to Angela and her family was real though, and if anything happened to any of them because of this crazy scheme, he'd never forgive himself. He didn't have any better ideas though and hey, it could even be fun. In the movies, the good guys always won, so surely they would this time as well, and the woman never got hurt. He would keep telling himself that.

Angela entertained Mattie for the remainder of the afternoon, while Luke and Jimmy went over their arrangements. They each had calls to make, and touched base occasionally to confirm each was on track.

Jimmy stayed for dinner and it was a novelty having the house full of guests, with lots of banter around the dining table. Luke knew Angela was making an effort for the benefit of her mother and son, but it made him conscious of how empty his house was at other times.

He had already retreated to his room after dinner when he heard footsteps come up the stairs, and the door to Angela's room opened and shut again. She had come up to bed. Stripping off his clothes, he stepped under the shower, letting the water jets massage the tension in his shoulders, all the while imagining her fingers massaging and kneading the knots away. By the time he stepped out of the shower, the household was quiet. He opened his bedroom door and listened, before padding down the hall.

Angela slipped naked between the sheets, watching the door in anticipation. She had itched to ask earlier if he was joining her, but suppressed the query. She reminded herself yet again—theirs was not a relationship in the conventional sense. It was a commercial arrangement which suited them both.

Realising finally he wasn't coming, she fell into a mortified and fitful sleep.

She had no idea how much later it was when she woke. *She wasn't alone*. Breath played rhythmically on the back of her neck and one arm was slung possessively over her, cupping a breast. She tensed initially in alarm, then relaxed again, allowing sleep to claim her once more.

7 – Exploring Options

Easing awake, Angela stretched languorously.

"Good morning, Miss Angelique." Luke was still beside her, propped on one elbow and watching her. His bed-tousled hair gave him a boyish look. She had an urge to reach out and run her hands through it. Instead, she wrapped her hands around his neck and drew him close enough that the few golden hairs on his chest tickled her breasts.

He responded with sliding a hand down her back until it came to rest on her butt. "I didn't have the heart to wake you," he said. "I've been watching you for a while. Did you know you make little snuffling noises while you sleep?"

She stared at him in astonishment, but not for long. His fingers began to dance a teasing pattern up one thigh, approaching sensitive territory.

"It's a big day, but a little morning glory might set the right tone, don't you think?" he murmured, throwing back the covers and exposing her body to the morning light. He leant over, delivering darting licks to first one nipple and then the other.

"But Mattie might come in. We could get sprung."

"Mm – we could. Spices things up a bit, doesn't it? I can be quick when I have to."

He directed little nibbles into the hollow at the top of her shoulders and up the side of her neck. His hand was continuing its own explorations, teasing and caressing. His cock had sprung to attention when the covers were thrown off, and now gently waved in response to his movements and exertions.

Angela arched back in response to his ministrations, now fully awake. Perhaps this would be her last opportunity – who knew what was going to happen to their relationship after today? Whatever, for now, she was taking charge. She used one foot against the bed to provide leverage and in a deft movement, flipped Luke over onto his back. He didn't have time to register confusion or surprise before she straddled him, delivering her own flickering kisses across his belly and over his torso. Her nipples, now erect, danced their own teasing path behind her tongue. She deftly ripped open the condom she'd conveniently slipped into the bedside drawer the day before, and slid it over the rigid member.

"Witch of a woman," he murmured. "Do you always wake up like this?"

She didn't answer but raising her body slightly, positioned his cock and slid the length of it into the warm, moist opening. She paused for a moment, savouring the sensation, before beginning a rhythmic movement, adjusting position and tempo for maximum effect. Grasping her hips, he followed her unspoken direction until moving in unison, first Angela then Luke exploded in shuddering ecstasy. He threw back his head in the throes of orgasmic delight, bucking upwards. Fearing he was about to add a vocal accompaniment, Angela quickly pressed her palm over his mouth, giggling as she did.

"Shh—they'll hear you."

"Right now, I don't care if they do." He caught her to him and held her against his chest while his ragged breathing was brought under control. It seemed for a while he was falling asleep. Watching the eyelashes fanned against his cheeks, and feeling his body start to relax, Angela knew she at least had to move. Time was passing, and Mattie must surely be stirring by now.

As soon as she started to manoeuvre herself gently off his body, his grip tightened, holding her there. "Where do you think you're going?"

"Into the shower for starters, and then probably to the kitchen. We can't stay here like this."

"Not sure why not, but if you must…" He released his grip and she slid out of bed, darting into the bathroom. By the time she was showered and out again, he'd gone. She hoped no one had seen him. That would be an unnecessary complication.

As Angela expected, Maria and her mother were already in the kitchen.

"You've got a spring in your step this morning," said Louise. "You must have slept well."

Angela could have sworn she saw her mother smirk. She wasn't about to ask why. Better to pretend she hadn't seen it. Instead she set about pouring a cup of coffee. Jimmy came into the kitchen, having stayed overnight too. She wondered how many bedrooms there were in the house.

"Are your plans all set for today?" Louise asked. "I hope you're not taking any unnecessary risks."

"It's all right, Mrs B. I'll be taking care of her."

"Thank you Jimmy, but don't you take any risks either."

Jimmy grinned good-naturedly and shrugged, insinuating life without risks would be boring.

Angela dropped some bread into the toaster. No doubt Maria would be working some sort of breakfast magic, but she wasn't that hungry.

"I wouldn't normally be seeing Stephen until one today, so until then I'll hang out here. Jimmy will drive me to the office before that, but there'll be a reception party keeping watch on access to the premises. Nobody will get close to me who shouldn't," Angela said to her mother.

Her phone pinged. A text arrived. *Wendy*. She was running ten minutes late but would pick Angela up shortly.

"Damn. I forgot to call Wendy. She's expecting me to accompany her today to visit another couple of salons. I'd better call her."

"Don't see why you can't still go," offered Jimmy. "I can drive you over to your place so she doesn't know where you're currently stayin' and I'll pick you up from there after she drops you home. I'll keep your place under observation until she arrives. What else are you goin' ter do this morning? Might as well make good use of your time."

114

"You're probably right." *Maybe then I won't think about what's going down today. What if guns are involved? Oh, God... what would happen to Mattie if I got shot? I can't let myself think about that.* She nodded at Jimmy. "Give me five minutes and I'll be ready to go."

She hurriedly confirmed arrangements with Wendy via text and was soon waiting at the front of her property, after quickly checking the letterbox for mail and watering a couple of pot plants. Jimmy had parked a discreet distance away, making sure that no unwelcome visitors arrived but within a few minutes, Wendy drew up in her Mazda.

Slipping into the passenger seat with a smile and a greeting, Angela noted that Wendy was not looking quite her previous perky self.

"Everything all right? You're looking a bit weary this morning." Haggard was more like it, but Angela wasn't going to say that.

"No, I'm fine. Just a few problems at home so I didn't sleep well last night."

"I'm sorry to hear that. Anything I can help with?"

"Not really, but thanks for asking."

No further information was volunteered so Angela let the subject drop, discussing instead the salons that were on the visiting list. Once again, Wendy reminded her she needed to get approval from the salon manager before Angela came inside, and some confidential discussions would be taken to a separate room.

"That's quite understood. I wouldn't expect anything less. I'm just so pleased to have this opportunity."

The managers of the two salons they visited were most generous with the information they were willing to impart. One of them recommended she consider joining the industry association, where she would learn a lot more.

"Thank you, I will. You've been so kind with your advice." *It's been a worthwhile morning, in more ways than one.*

Throughout the morning, she was conscious that Wendy still seemed troubled, but perhaps after a good night's sleep that would pass. Hopefully it was nothing too serious. They chattered about inconsequential matters in the car on the way back to Angela's house.

"Are you married?" Wendy asked.

"I was briefly. I've been on my own for a long time now."

"Life can be simpler that way. There's a lot to be said for only having responsibility for yourself and your own decisions."

There was a reflective silence.

"Sorry I've been reserved today," Wendy continued. "I've just discovered my husband has slipped back into old gambling habits. I think he's in real trouble."

"Oh, wow. I'm not surprised you're upset. Can you get help from Gamblers Anonymous or some similar organisation?"

"It might be too late for that." Wendy thumped the steering wheel with a clenched fist. "He promised me this wouldn't happen again, he promised! I'm scared we'll lose the house. If his employer learns what he's done, the fall-out will be significant. He says he has a plan, but I've heard that

116

before. On top of other family issues, it's the last thing we need right now."

"Wendy, I'm so sorry to hear that. Can you transfer the house to your name? It sounds as though you should be making some plans of your own. It's a lesson I learnt years ago – never depend financially on anyone else. It puts you in a very vulnerable position."

"Now she tells me!" Wendy glanced at her with a wry smile. "Sorry to dump on you—I felt I would explode if I didn't tell someone."

She pulled up outside Angela's house. Jimmy was already parked discreetly a short distance up the road where he could observe their arrival.

"Feel free to dump on me any time. You've been a big help to me this week; I'm more than happy to provide a listening ear. Let me know if I can help in any way." Angela waved Wendy off with a tinge of sadness. Although the early years after her husband left had been tough, she appreciated the freedom and independence that came with it. She was glad not to have Wendy's problems.

Against usual practice, she sat in the front seat with Jimmy. They were travelling directly to the apartment, and she wanted the security of his close presence.

"Everything and everyone's in place, Miss Angelique. The plan has been tested from every angle, so you don't have to worry. They'll see Luke aka Mr Lundy arrive, and he'll come up in the elevator. He'll stay with you. All you have to do is respond appropriately when you're contacted. The only concern I have is that they might smell a rat and back out before we've got them cornered. We have to make sure everything looks as normal as possible."

"You still haven't told me. What are you going to do once you've intercepted these men? What if they're armed?"

"If they are, they won't be the only ones, but this will be a coercive rather than violent action. We have a van ready to pick them up. It will follow them into the carpark after a small interval, ensuring they can't make a run for it. After they've been restrained, we'll transport them to a secure place where we can interrogate them. Best if you don't know any more than that."

Jimmy was probably right. He seemed so confident, but Angela was twitchy all the same. To distract herself, she rang Sasha from the car to report on her morning tour.

"It's been so helpful, Sasha. I've dropped some ideas and picked up a few others. I'm more convinced that this will be my next venture. Recent events have moved my plans along; I'm glad you introduced me to Sheldon. Wendy has been a great source of information as well."

"Yes, she's a lovely woman. I've met her a couple of times."

"With Sheldon?"

"No, she has accompanied her husband. I don't think she really needs to work; after all he has a high-powered job. His income must be substantial."

"She didn't tell me what her husband did, and I didn't ask. I was more focussed on the salons."

"Her husband is David Cornell. I believe I introduced him to you some months back."

118

Wendy! Angela felt a flush of embarrassment. She had not met the wife of one of her clients before. They were shadowy figures in the background and she didn't need to know anything about them. She and Wendy had met on a first name basis, so she hadn't made the connection.

This was one more reason for choosing a new business opportunity. She wasn't sure she could look Wendy in the eye again. Thank goodness they didn't have any more salon visits scheduled. She resolved to send Wendy a small gift as a thank you.

Inside the apartment, there was no need to transition from Angela into Angelique, so she stayed dressed as she was. She had some time before the action was likely to start. She made herself a cup of coffee and fired up the laptop. At least she could review her spreadsheet-based feasibility study, feeding in some of the new information she'd gleaned.

It was difficult to focus, as her mind kept wandering back over the events of the week. She kept seeing Mattie's white face as he peered down from the top of the stairs, scared by what he'd just witnessed. If anyone every harmed her sweet child, she'd tear them apart herself.

She glanced at her watch. Not long to go. She rang her mother.

"Are you okay, mum?"

"Yes, dear. We're both fine. When this is all over though, I'd like to know a bit more about what has been going on."

"There's not a lot I can tell as I'm confused myself. At least we're all safe and that's the main thing. See you later this afternoon. Love you." *Love Mattie too.*

She hung up before her mother could press her any further. She had to think about what version of events she was going to give Louise. It needed to be an edited account and hopefully omitting details about Angelique. She would focus on future plans for the salon instead.

The next decision was what to do about Angelique's clients. She had a feeling that Mr Thursday and Mr Friday had dropped off the calendar. The nature of her relationship with Luke Johnson had changed. She repressed the inner voice of protest. Best she quietly terminates that booking though losing him didn't bear thinking about. As far as Friday went, probably Stephen Lundy would make the decision himself. He would no longer see her as a safe haven.

That left Mr Monday, Tuesday and Wednesday. She hoped none of them got wind of current events, or she wouldn't be left with any clients. She needed to maintain a certain level of income while putting future plans into action. Unless something went drastically wrong, there was no need for those three to learn of the week's drama. Stephen wouldn't talk and she doubted Luke would either.

Her thoughts turned to David Cornell. According to Wendy, he was in financial strife. That didn't sound right. A man in his position wouldn't be so stupid, would he? Surely Sasha would have known and told her if he was a gambler. When you got to know people in one facet of their lives, you never knew what was going on in the other areas. She felt so sorry for Wendy.

Luke called from the car. He was approaching the car park.

"No sign of any black Volvo. If they're here, they'll have noted my approach."

"Okay, check the car park carefully and if you're sure no-one is hiding in a corner, ping me and I'll send the elevator down."

"Jimmy assures me he's done a thorough sweep of the basement and also the cars that are already parked, so it should be fine. See you soon."

She was relieved when the elevator doors opened to the lobby, and the peep-hole in the door revealed Luke to be on the other side. Importantly, he was alone. No masked men or other intruders. She had the urge to throw open the door, pull him inside and slam it again before anyone else could push in behind him, but that was silly. He had taken precautions.

"What?" he queried as she opened the door. "I was expecting to be greeted by Angelique, temptress extraordinaire."

"Sorry, you've got Plain Jane Angela. Angelique is taking a hiatus."

"That's not the way it seemed this morning. That was a helluva way to wake up. Nothing like a woman who takes control."

She had a feeling that not many women had taken control where Luke Johnson was concerned, unless it was his mother, and that was probably when he was in short pants.

"Make the most of it while it lasts, Sugar," she purred at him, running a well-manicured fingernail down his chest. "With a bit of luck, this will all be over this afternoon and then Mattie, Mother and I will be out of your hair."

He caught her hand before it went too far, and dropped a light kiss on her forehead.

"We'll talk about that later. I wish you had CCTV monitoring up here. I want to know what's happening downstairs. I caught a glimpse of Lundy across the road with the painting team, under a cap and wearing big sunglasses. The overalls looked lovely on him as well."

"Luke, there's no need for sarcasm. Stephen is charming when you get to know him."

"I doubt I'll ever know him in quite the same way you do." His tone was now flat. This was getting into dangerous territory. She needed a change of topic.

"Tell me about your coming trip. Where are you going and what are you hoping to achieve?"

The look he gave her indicated he was aware of her strategy but he provided a brief synopsis of his itinerary, and the products he was hoping to demonstrate in each country. He didn't get far before a text arrived on his phone. It was from Jimmy.

We're on.

Angela's heart began to thud. She hoped she sounded confident, without a tremor in her voice. Then her phone rang. It was her work phone, the one used by Angelique. She locked eyes with Luke for a moment before picking it up and connecting the call.

"Hello?"

A low-pitched voice answered. The accent appeared to be Australian. Definitely no Asian triads here.

"Good morning, Miss Angelique. This is no time for funny business. Give me the code to access the car park.

We'll be out of your hair shortly and you and your family will be safe."

"How did you get this number? Who gave it to you?"

The voice on the other end rose a notch. "We're not here to chat. Give me the code! Stay on the line."

Luke was close enough to hear this exchange, and gave her a nod.

She dictated the code, and could hear a murmur of voices in the background. She wondered how many men were there. She heard the beeping of the keypad and then the grinding noise as the door slid open.

Luke was monitoring the response action on his own phone. Angela wasn't sure what was happening, but he gave her the thumbs up.

"Okay, Angelique. We're at the elevator; bring us up." The voice was curt.

She hit the button on her security console and waited. She heard a 'bing' as the elevator doors opened, then the connection was broken. She had no way of knowing what was happening.

Luke turned his phone off, and ran for the door.

"Stay here. It sounds like a bit of a barney down there. I'm going down to help."

"There's only one lift. If I bring it up, they might still be in it." She tried to control the panic in her voice.

"You're right. I'll take the stairs. Lock the door behind me and don't let anyone in unless it's Jimmy or me."

Angela heard the fire door slam, and then nothing. She cocked her head straining to hear what was happening. Anything. The waiting was excruciating. She reached a hand towards the door knob and then dropped it again. She was tempted to take the fire stairs herself, but didn't want Jimmy's team feeling they had to protect her at the expense of securing the men. She crossed to the windows in the vain hope that she could see something out there. She didn't expect to as her view was only of the harbour. As usual, there was a smattering of yachts on the water and two men zoomed past on jet skis. They were noisy. Those things should be banned.

There was a small jetty and mooring facility attached to the apartment complex, but not having a boat, she didn't go down there often. Only when she wanted some fresh air and a change of scenery. Now there was a sizable vessel moored at the end. She hadn't seen it before and wondered which of her neighbours owned it. A figure emerged from the cabin and stood, hands on hips, looking up at her windows. A band tightened around her chest. Who was it?

She kept a pair of binoculars on the window sill for those times when she wanted a closer look at river activities. This was one of them. Standing to one side where she was confident a watcher couldn't see her, Angela raised the binoculars to her eyes. She didn't need to really. It was just confirmation. The body shape and the stance was familiar to her. Still, she had to be sure.

Grabbing her phone, she quickly dialled Luke and he answered immediately.

"I know who it is. I know who's behind it. His boat is moored at the jetty, ready for a getaway."

The man was David Cornell—Mr Wednesday.

8 – Guess Who?

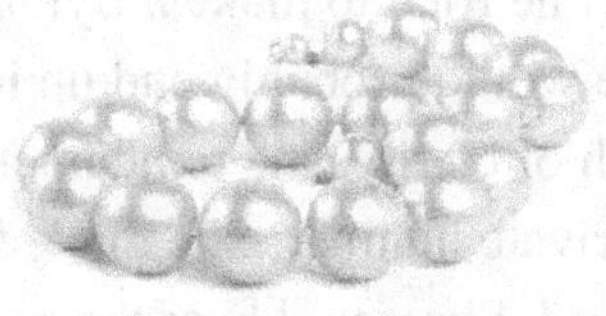

Something must have alerted David Cornell his scheme was starting to unravel. He sprang up, untying the mooring rope and pushing off from the jetty. Angela ran out onto the balcony and heard the engine start.

"David!" she screamed. "I know it's you. Come back!"

It was futile. There was no way he would hear her over the engine from five floors up, and even if he did, he was clearly a desperate man. She saw Luke run out along the jetty, signalling wildly to the two men on the jet skis. They swung in close. Next thing, the two machines took off again, this time with Luke riding pillion on the back of one.

"Follow that boat," Angela muttered under her breath. "What does he think he's playing at?" She watched the chase unfolding across the water. "They must all think they're in the middle of a James Bond movie."

She raised the binoculars again. The jet skis were drawing close, but were nearing a bend in the coastline. Once they were behind that, she wouldn't be able to see a thing.

As predicted, moments later, the boat had disappeared and the jet skis behind it. All she could see was the wake left in their path. How did Luke think he was going to stop the boat, anyway? If he tried to make a flying leap from the back of the jet ski, he would probably end up in the water.

With a flash of clarity, she remembered she had Mr Wednesday's private number. She dialled and was surprised when he answered. She could hear the noise of the boat in the background and shouted in the hope that he could hear her.

"David, it's Angelique! You need to turn around and come back. I know you're in trouble. Let's talk about how we can help you."

"I can't do that, Angelique. I'm in too deep. My options are limited."

His words caused a stab of panic. He sounded despairing. Surely he wouldn't see self-harm as an answer? If anyone was going to kill him, it should be her. After that, probably his wife would be in the queue.

"David, think about what you're doing to Wendy. She doesn't deserve this. Come back, please."

"What do you know about Wendy? She's nothing to do with you."

"David, she's my friend, and so are you. Please come back. Your scheme has gone pear-shaped. Don't do anything stupid. She wants you home."

She crossed her fingers behind her back hoping that was true. She heard the engine decelerate which surely meant

David was slowing down in preparation for turning around. She returned inside, shutting the sliding door and headed for the elevator. It seemed to take forever before the doors opened and the elevator took her down to ground level. Assuming Jimmy had things under control in the basement car park, she headed outside and ran around the building to the jetty at the water's edge.

She was in time to see the motor launch rounding the cove and followed by the two jet skis, and heading for the jetty. Luke was at the wheel of the boat, so he'd evidently pulled off a James Bond stunt after all. As he jumped onto the jetty to secure the mooring rope, Angela clambered on and made her way to David. The big man she had come to know seemed to have shrunk. Was it only two days ago he'd been in her bed, joking and carrying on as if he had not a care in the world? His involvement in this debacle was confusing. Her first instinct was to throttle him, but that would have to wait. First, to get him off the boat.

She put her arms around him in a hug. "Come upstairs with me, David. Tell me what's happened and what's pushed you to this."

She caught Luke's eye, indicating that for now, she had it under control. He waved off the jet ski boys before following them. Angela wasn't sure but she thought she might have glimpsed money changing hands.

They were waiting for the elevator in the foyer, when the main door to the street opened, and there stood Stephen, still in his painter's disguise. David didn't pay him any attention until Stephen spoke.

"Who are you, and why me?"

David looked around in confusion, peering at the overall-clad figure standing before him. Stephen removed his sunglasses and cap, worn rapper-style backwards. There was an expectant silence as everyone looked at David, who now had an ashen pallor.

"Lundy! I wasn't expecting to see you."

"I don't see why not. I thought getting hold of me was what it was all about, or were you just going to let your goons deal with me while you remained at a distance?"

"I don't think this is the place to discuss this," interjected Angela smoothly. "Why don't we go upstairs where we can sit down? I think we all might need a drink."

She had misgivings about inviting them all into her domain but it was more apparent than ever that its previous use was rapidly coming to an end. Mr Wednesday would no longer be an option, and that only left Mr Monday and Mr Tuesday, and she couldn't survive if she relied only on them. Either she had to find some new clients very fast or resort to plan B. As it seemed her cover had easily been blown, maintaining her role as Angelique would not be easy.

"Where's Jimmy?" she asked. Having his solid presence upstairs would be a good idea. He could control any aggression or unpleasant behaviour. The apartment was her territory, and all of the men would be cognisant of the fact that there, she made the rules. At least she had done in the past, and she was going to keep doing so while she could.

"Jimmy's down in the basement with the heavies." Stephen didn't attempt to hide his derision, his confidence growing now the danger was past. As they all stepped into the elevator, Angela dialled Jimmy on her phone.

"Jimmy, can your mates take care of matters down there? I'd like you to join us upstairs."

Luke looked at her, one eyebrow raised in query. Angela knew he thought he could take care of things, but she wanted the security of Jimmy's presence. She avoided eye contact with Luke. She had to if she was to maintain control of the situation.

David seemed to realise he had no option other than to cooperate. Once they entered the apartment, he moved to the sliding door to the balcony and stood looking out. He looked so broken and desolate that Angela wondered if he was contemplating making a dash for the parapet and throwing himself over. Luke must have thought the same, as he quickly removed the key from the door lock.

Stephen was just angry. He didn't say as much but the emotion emanated from every pore. His posture was stiff, and he stood, arms crossed, staring at David. Wearing the workman's overalls seemed to give him permission to deviate from his usual polite and accommodating behaviour.

Angela glanced at each of them. "Anyone for a drink? I should be able to cater for most choices. David, you look like you could do with a Whiskey."

"You know me too well, darling girl." He gave her an apologetic smile, as she opened her drinks cabinet and took their orders. Jimmy's arrival caused momentary distraction, giving Angela an opportunity to discreetly close the bedroom door.

With drinks sorted, she invited them all to take a seat at the dining table. Jimmy was the only one who remained standing, his stance suggesting anyone who tried any funny business wouldn't get away with it. None of the men looked happy sitting down together, but did as she instructed.

Angela took the lead. "David, what the fuck? You betrayed me and my trust in you. How dare you endanger those close to me! What you were trying to achieve with this little stunt?"

"Little!" interrupted Stephen. "I don't think that plotting to kidnap me and threaten your family is a little stunt."

Be quiet, Stephen. I've got this. Angela held up her hand, palm outwards, to silence the outburst, maintaining eye contact with the man who shrank before the intensity of her glare. Now that the danger appeared to be over, her repressed anger erupted. "The whole operation was so amateurish. You've been incredibly stupid—for a financier, even more so. Why did you pick on Stephen?"

"Well, it was his father, really. Lundy Junior was just collateral damage."

"Don't bullshit. How is his father involved with this?"

"I wanted Paul Lundy to know what it was like to lose a child. I wanted him to feel helpless and to suffer anguish. I wanted *him* to experience the full impact of his actions and decisions."

"What has my father ever done to you?" asked Stephen, not hiding his confusion.

"He's devoid of any vestige of humanity."

Luke had been silent so far but now he entered the conversation.

"Cut the diatribe, Cornell. and give us the facts. Go back to the beginning and explain what you were trying to achieve and why. We haven't got all day, and keep in mind, what we decide to do with you will depend on your answer."

David turned to look at Angela. "You said you know Wendy. I'm confused as to how that has come about, but did she tell you about Melanie?"

"No. Who's Melanie?"

"Melanie is our daughter. She was mad keen on horses as a kid, but she had a bad fall one day resulting in T10 spinal damage. She's a paraplegic, being paralysed from the waist down and gets around in a wheelchair instead of on a horse these days. She's desperate to walk again and to have the life she might have expected as a young woman."

He didn't look at them, but stared down at the table, his voice a weary monotone. "Wendy and I have exhausted all management options in Australia, but we heard about a revolutionary new treatment in California. Not everyone is eligible, depending on the extent of the damage, but Wendy and Melanie were keen to get into one of the trials."

"I'm sorry about your daughter, Cornell, but I don't see this has anything with me. I didn't make her fall off the horse, and neither did my father." Stephen dropped his face into his open palms, rubbing at his temples. Angela was bemused to note the speckles of paint on the backs of his hands. It would be rare for him to do any manual work. Good for him to get some experience of how the other half lived.

"The accident was nobody's fault, but it has had broad impacts on all of us as a family unit." David paused before continuing. "I've recently become fiscally embarrassed, to phrase it nicely. It prompted me to do something really stupid. I would never have considered it if it weren't for Melanie. Even just thinking about it, I'm ashamed."

"Stop beating about the bush and fess up to what you've done," suggested Luke. "We don't have all day.

The look David gave him was baleful. He sighed and bit his lip before continuing in a quieter voice than before. He avoided eye contact with anyone as he spoke, looking instead through the window to the harbour beyond.

"I had some of the money I needed to send Melanie and Wendy to the States, but paying for the treatment and all the specialists, plus funding their living expenses for six months at least, was going to take a lot. More than I had. I was desperate. Wendy was relying on me, and I couldn't let my daughter down. This could be her last opportunity to improve her condition. I've had luck at the tables before—mostly Blackjack as I've got a good memory for figures—and thought if I could just double my money, the problem would be solved."

Angela shook her head in disbelief. Where was the man who'd given her sound financial advice on more than one occasion?

"Stress got the better of me this time and I lost the lot, and more. I've known Paul Lundy for years—we go way back—and I asked him for a line of credit. He turned me down. He wouldn't give me one. My back was against the wall and there only seemed one option left. I manipulated some transactions at work, and obtained the money that way—and then I lost that too."

"That's embezzlement," Angela said, unable to hide her amazement. "David, what were you thinking?"

132

"Of course, my father turned you down," interjected Stephen. "He's a businessman, not a player on the short-term money market. He takes a black and white view on gambling. It's your choice. Never bet with more than you can afford to lose." He sat back with folded arms. "Anyway, the casinos are my domain, not my father's."

David sat forward and thumped his hands on the table. "He was callous. He didn't care he was condemning my daughter to a life in a wheelchair. I wanted him to know what it feels like when your family is under threat."

"You're a fool. Has it occurred to you that if you had approached my father for help in the first place, explaining your daughter's situation instead of asking for a line of credit to gamble, he would probably have helped you out? There was no need to throw everything away at the casino."

"A man's got some pride. I didn't want to go cap-in-hand, asking for help. I should be able to provide for my own daughter's needs."

"So where do I come into this little escapade?"

"I wanted him to know what it feels like to have a child under threat, even though you're significantly older than my Melanie. I arranged for a tail to be put on you, and was surprised when I discovered you were in receipt of Executive Coaching from Angelique."

Angela coloured and avoided looking at Luke. She kept her focus on Stephen.

"I only formulated my plan after learning of this. I was simply going to hold you captive until your father coughed up with a ransom. I knew he wouldn't go to the police. He's as publicity shy as I am, and there are a few skeletons rattling

133

in his closet as well. I know about them and he knows I know."

Angela was embarrassed at the revelations. It was all so sad and tawdry. This was not funny. Glancing up, she saw Luke looking at her with a frown on his face. Was that frown because he was thinking about her and all he'd learnt in recent days? She hoped his disapproval was directed at the whole sorry situation, rather than her.

Realising she was looking at him, Luke gave a quick conspiratorial wink before addressing those at the table. "Enough talk. First we need to deal with the goons, as Lundy calls them. As they were just the hired help, I suggest we take their photos and copies of any ID they have, plus the car registration and send them on their way. Jimmy can put the word out in his network. If any of those men are seen in this vicinity again, they'll be dealt with. If only one turns up, the others will pay. We'll be able to find them if we want to. Agreed?"

There was consensus, except from David, who understandably remained silent. The next question would be what they proposed to do with him. Jimmy moved briefly to one side and made a phone call. Presumably he was issuing instructions to his associates in the car park.

Luke turned to David. "There's no denying you've been a total fool, but I don't see that your wife and daughter should suffer because of your incompetence. It wasn't exactly a sophisticated plan. By chance, I have a condominium in San Francisco, and I can make it available to them if they get themselves to the States. That takes care of some of the living expenses."

134

"But that still leaves the treatment. I don't have the money for that anymore."

Luke looked at Stephen. "Lundy? Can you come up with some of the readies?"

"Me? You're joking, aren't you? Why would I do anything to help this man, let alone provide him with money? We've already seen what he's done with his own funds. It would be just throwing good money after bad."

Angela was surprised at the direction in the conversation was taking. She topped up Stephen's drink. He looked as though he needed it.

"You don't have any kids, do you?" Luke asked.

"I don't. I'm not married either. Usually the two go together."

"Perhaps when you *do* become a father, you'll understand the emotional pressure to do whatever you can when they're hurting."

Did Luke have children? He hadn't mentioned it, but there was obviously a child who'd stayed at the house.

"Look, I can't let you do this. My financial problems are nothing to do with you."

David had stopped gazing through the window and looked at each of them. "I'll sell the house; I'll sell everything. I'll get the money somehow."

"Your financial problems are everything to do with me." Stephen didn't hide his anger. "How can you plot my kidnapping, and ask my father for ransom without appreciating that your financial problems are now everything to do with me?"

David had the good grace to look embarrassed. Angela topped up his drink as well. She topped up Luke's glass, but Jimmy declined. He didn't like drinking when he was 'on the job'.

"I'll tell you what I'll do," said Stephen. "My mother runs a charitable foundation. I'll put it to her that she suggest to the directors they assist your wife and daughter. No guarantees and I don't know how much the foundation will provide. They will want some detailed information, but presumably that's not a problem."

"Stephen, under the circumstances, that would be a wonderful offer. David, I wish you'd asked for help before this. You could have spoken to me!" Angelique said.

"No Angelique; that wouldn't have been appropriate."

"I don't have the resources to directly help you, but I do know a lot of influential people who could."

David bowed his head. "I'm truly grateful for what you are all suggesting. I never meant for any of this to happen, you must understand that. I was so desperate, I wasn't thinking straight. I still have to deal with the situation I've created at work, but at least if Melanie can access the treatment, that will be a load off my mind."

Luke spoke up again. "As far as your embezzlement issues go, you're on your own. It's up to you whether you sell off your assets, or man-up to what you've done, because I for one am not interested."

"You're not suggesting we just let him go are you? Where's the justice in that? He hasn't disclosed what he was intending to do with me, for how long, or where." Stephen's fingers turned white where he gripped the edges of the table.

136

His nostrils flared as he leaned forward and fixed David with a deadly stare, causing the other man to sit back slightly.

"I wasn't going to cut your ear off, or anything like that," protested David. "You'd have been quite comfortable. I was just going to keep you sedated, and hidden securely on the boat until your father came to the party."

"Oh, well that's just fine then," sneered Stephen. "No problem at all."

Angela knew she needed to diffuse the rising hostility if they were to reach any decisions. Stephen needed to be appeased. She directed her attention to him.

"Were you suggesting we involve the police? They'll ask lots of questions of course—what the connection is between the two of you; why you come here; what the issue is that David knows about your father… Do you want them investigating your private lives and the media getting hold of it as well?"

"No, of course not."

"If you think David's getting off scot-free, that won't be the case. He'll have to answer to the auditors at the bank and at the very least, will lose his job. He'll also have to sell off assets to make restitution. He'll be dealing with the consequences of his actions and everything that led up to it."

She turned to look at Jimmy, still standing but listening intently. He was the only one who had remained silent.

"What's your view, Jimmy? What do you think is an appropriate course of action?"

The big man cleared his throat before speaking. "The goons won't trouble us again; I've made sure of that. From what I've heard, Mr Cornell is unlikely to bother us again either. On the other hand, I'm angry that Mrs B and young Matthew were threatened, but hopefully there's no long term damage there. I reckon he's brought punishment on himself with his stupid actions. We can safely let him go."

"Are you both agreed?"

Angela looked at Luke and Stephen. They both nodded, though Stephen still didn't look happy. She didn't have the patience to pander to him any more than she did with David Cornell.

She stood up. "I've had enough excitement for one day. If there's nothing else to discuss, I'd like to assure my family there is no further danger and that we can all go home."

Stephen also stood, and looked around, almost as though looking at the room for the first time. Watching him, Angela realised it was probably for the last time.

"I'll take myself off," he said. "I don't think there's anything more to be gained today. I assume I won't be followed or accosted on the way home?"

This last comment was directed at David, who gave a small shake of his head. Neither man sought eye contact. With a nod to the group, Stephen turned abruptly and left, shutting the door firmly behind him. Angela sighed. She supposed she couldn't blame him for some petulance.

David stood hesitantly, unsure of whether he was really free to go. Luke held up the keys to the boat.

"As you came on the boat, I assume that's the way you'll go. You'll need these. I'll be in touch about the matters we discussed."

David grabbed the keys, and with a softly muttered apology, bolted for the door. Angela moved to shut it behind

138

him. Her words were directed softly, just for his ears. "David—I don't think you require any further coaching, do you?"

She didn't wait for a response, shutting the door and turning back to Luke and Jimmy.

"I'll just wash the glasses and tidy up here, and I'll be ready to go. Jimmy, will you be able to drive my mother and myself home after we've had time to pack our things?"

"Of course. If Mr Johnson is driving you back to his home, I'll just see that Mr Cornell gets away and check there are no more surprises downstairs."

~

The ache in his jaw made Luke aware he'd been clenching his teeth. He walked to the window and looked out at the scene below. David Cornell walked along the jetty and untied the mooring rope before jumping onto his boat. A few moments later, it pulled away and was soon out of sight. Another of her clients. How many more were there?

He was glad the door to the bedroom was shut. He didn't want his memories of that time sullied with mental images of Angelique with either Lundy or Cornell. He knew he hadn't gone into the arrangement naively. When her attention focused on him, and that hot body of hers wrapped around his, it was easy to forget that for Angelique, it was a commercial transaction. He was a fool and with nobody to blame but himself.

He'd allowed himself to think they were developing something tangible. He'd given her the opportunity to back out while she was in his house, but she was the one who had initiated the day's morning glory. She probably thought of it as payment for services rendered.

The sooner he was on that plane and out of the country the better. Perhaps then the hollow feeling in the depths of his gut would disappear.

~

It didn't take Angela long to tidy the apartment. Luke remained uncharacteristically silent throughout, standing by the partially opened sliding door to the balcony and watching activity on the harbour below. It wasn't until they were later in the car that he turned to her, an enigmatic expression on his face.

"So, Angelique; who else has been on the receiving end of Executive Coaching?"

9 – An End to Executive Coaching

Angela stiffened. He wasn't supposed to ask these questions. He must know that. "Surely you understand the issue of client confidentiality. I can't talk about my clients or disclose anything about them."

"Ah… your clients. Obviously, there was Lundy and Cornell besides myself. I'm assuming there were others."

"Luke, why are you bringing this up now? You never asked before. You must have understood there were other clients in my life."

"I guess I took the head in the sand approach. When it seemed we had a special connection, it was easy to ignore what else your life entailed."

The feeling of dread that had threatened for a while now rose briefly to the surface, and then plunged to the pit of her belly. Angela felt sick. She'd expected some sort of reaction from him but at the same time, hoped it wouldn't happen.

What was there left to say? She looked out of the window, anywhere rather than at him. Whatever happened, she didn't want Luke Johnson to know how distressed she was. Control. She had to maintain self-control.

The rest of the journey was conducted in silence and it was a relief when the gates swung open and they pulled into the drive.

Mattie rushed outside to meet them when he heard the car pull up.

"Luke—do you want to see what I made?" He was holding a Lego masterpiece, which must have kept him busy for a while. "I've had the best day. Maria made pancakes again, and then we had a swim in the pool."

Besides Jimmy, there were no men in the small boy's life and Angela noted with sadness that Mattie was gravitating towards Luke. She needed to go home quickly before Mattie became too attached. There was nothing to be gained from that except heartache. It was bad enough dealing with her own distress without dealing with his.

"Mattie, you need to put everything back where you found it and pack up your things. We're going home tonight. I'm not surprised you've had a good time, but it's back to school for you on Monday."

"But Mum, I like it here. I thought you said it wasn't safe at home?"

Luke had been standing by silently, but now addressed the boy. "That's a really cool plane. If you want, you can take it with you. We've found the bad guys who threatened you and your Nan the other day and they won't bother you again."

142

Matthew gave him a doubtful look, but the prospect of taking his plane with him over-rode any negative emotions.

"You didn't have to do that, but thank you," Angela said stiffly. "I'd better find my mother."

As she had anticipated, Louise was in the kitchen with Maria.

"Hi sweetheart," Louise said. "Jimmy gave me the good news. I don't have the detail, but I gather you've found those hoodlums and we're no longer in any danger."

"You've heard right, Mum. We can go home. It's a long and somewhat sad story, but we know who was behind the threat to Stephen Lundy and I'm sure he won't bother us again. I'll pack up my things and as soon as you're ready too, we can go."

"You can't go before dinner," interrupted Maria. "I've prepared a celebratory meal and your mother has helped. It's the regional speciality from my home country. I have been teaching your mother how to cook it."

"It's been lovely to have the company," Louise said wistfully. "I've enjoyed my time with Maria, and we've arranged to meet up for coffee next week."

Angela could feel several sets of eyes looking at her, including Luke's. She couldn't ignore him any longer. She sighed and turned to him. Part of her wanted to stay longer as well.

"I feel we shouldn't impose on you any further, but I think I'm on the losing end of the debate here. Is it okay with you if we leave after dinner?"

She couldn't read the look he gave her. He was just being polite. He was probably as keen for her to be gone as she was to be out of his hair and back into her own space. He was always polite in front of the older women though.

"Of course. Where's Jimmy? He should be in on this celebration as well. I can vouch for Maria's cooking," Luke said.

It was Louise who answered. "He insisted on doing a tour of the property and local streets. He never quite switches off. He should be back soon."

On cue, Jimmy entered through the back door, giving a thumbs-up. "No loose ends that I could see. We're free to go."

The collar of his jacket was turned up, and he was wearing running shoes, presumably to move quickly if necessary. Angela felt a surge of affection for the man. She'd be so lost without him.

"You don't mind staying for dinner first, do you, Jimmy?" Louise asked.

"If dinner is what I can smell, I'd be a fool to turn that down. I'll go and wash up first."

Maria's cooking was all that was promised, and more. A steaming dish of Chicken Cacciatore along with platters of braised broccolini and roasted rosemary potatoes were placed on the table for everyone to help themselves, with slices of her home-made bread 'made the way my Nona taught me'. Jimmy was particularly appreciative, and entertained the table with stories of the meals from his childhood. Such was his bonhomie he even promised to demonstrate his own culinary talents at some unspecified time. If the others noticed the reserve between Luke and Angela, they didn't comment.

144

As soon as was reasonable, Angela excused herself from the table, and went to the room she'd been using to pack up her toiletries and other bits and pieces. She felt his presence before she saw him.

"So what now?" Luke asked. "Angelique continues coaching as before?"

He leant against the doorframe, arms crossed, watching as she moved around the bedroom gathering up her things. She hadn't told him about her salon concept, and was reluctant to say anything until she had greater certainty about her idea. She didn't want to jinx the project before it had really started, and if she were honest with herself, she preferred that she was up and running and able to prove herself as a competent business woman before sharing her idea with him.

"I've got a few things to consider, but I'm not without options. I understand that our Thursday appointment will not be continuing. You'll probably want to seek your executive coaching elsewhere."

"Executive coaching..." It was a pause that spoke volumes. " ...well, you're creative Angelique, I'll give you that, and your technique is faultless. How many 'clients' have you had to develop that level of expertise?" His words were cutting and she felt the pain of each one.

Angela straightened and turned to face him, hands on hips. "How dare you sneer at me? You were happy to utilise my services. I never had any complaints from you. Quite the opposite. You entered our arrangement with your eyes open."

"That I did. It turned out a little differently to what I expected. I'm not sneering; there was nothing to criticise about those Thursday afternoons; far from it. I'll shortly leave for my trip to the Middle East, so any form of executive coaching won't be happening for a while." His eyes were hooded, hiding what he might be thinking. "The break will probably do me good."

She was momentarily desolated. With everything that had occurred in the last couple of days, she'd forgotten he was going away. Not only was she leaving his house, but he was not even going to be in the country. There would be little justifiable reason to see him again when he returned. At least she could try to leave on good terms. *This is awkward. How do I manage this?*

"Luke, I haven't thanked you for all you've done. You didn't have to take us all in; it was nothing to do with you really." She raised her eyes to his. "I appreciate what you've done for us. I hope your trip is successful. Once we're out of your hair, you can focus on your preparations."

"Do you honestly think you'll ever be 'out of my hair', as you put it?" He reached out and pulled her roughly to him nearly causing her to over-balance. With a hand entwined in her hair, he pulled her head back so that she looked up at him. Her initial response was to attempt to push away from him, but his grip was too strong. His heart beat a tom-tom against her chest, with a matching response from hers. The aftershave she had learned to associate with him assailed her nostrils. Her initial resistance melted as he pulled her closer and claimed her lips with a savagery that left her breathless.

Releasing her hair, his hand slid down her back, dancing a journey that evoked a corresponding fandango on the inside. His hard length pressed against her. There was no hiding the intensity of his desire. Her body began to respond with its own primeval dance, taking over her pulse and her heated emotions. How could this man have such a mesmerising effect on her?

This is ridiculous, she thought. *There's no future in this.*

With an inner strength that surprised them both, she pushed him away.

"Jimmy will be waiting," she said, her voice still husky. "It's time I left." She pushed back the hair which had flopped over her face in an effort to regain her composure.

"You probably should, but I'm not ready to let this go. You can't deny what we have between us. Perhaps we can come to some arrangement on my return?"

"I don't think so Luke. I'm nobody's play thing. We had a business arrangement in the past but there have been changes in the last week and there'll be more changes in weeks to come. My focus now is on my son and our future."

Ignoring his stony-faced response, she turned and fled to the ensuite bathroom and closed the door. She looked at herself in the mirror, not recognising the woman who stared back. There was a wildness about her eyes, and an air of apprehension.

When she emerged, he'd gone. There was a resultant chill in the room, and she quickly gathered her overnight bag and toiletries and joined the others in the kitchen. Jimmy was just finishing a cup of coffee and was ready to go. There were some final protests from Mattie, but even he looked forward to being back home, and being able to tell his mates all about his 'holiday'.

Maria gave them all a big hug, and extracted promises from them to come back again. "This house is big – it needs a family. You must come and eat at my table again."

The weekend entailed the usual domesticity and parental chores. Matthew had soccer, and Angela sat on the sidelines with the other mums, cheering him on. She had no idea what the game was about, and suspected that a significant number of the kids didn't either but they enjoyed themselves while their coach ran up and down on the sidelines, trying to instil some cohesive ball skills in his young charges.

She took the opportunity to give Sasha a quick call, updating her on the previous day's events.

"Sasha, that immediate problem is solved, but otherwise, my life has gone pear-shaped. I've lost three clients in the space of a day. My cover is blown, and my relationship with those three has changed. I'm not quite ready to progress the salon idea, but trying to survive with my remaining two clients is not viable either."

The older woman was sympathetic. "It's good news you're all safe again, but losing those clients is a problem. I'm sure it is only a short-term hiatus. I've a couple of functions to attend with Renato this week. If I see any prospects of interest, I'll let you know. You can take it from there."

"Thanks Sasha; I don't know what I'd do without you both."

The trouble was, Angela wasn't sure if she really wanted new clients. Now she'd started thinking about new business opportunities, she was anxious to progress that idea. To take more executive coaching clients seemed a backwards step. It might be a financial necessity though.

Mattie came running over, signalling the end of the game. "Mum, can we have a hamburger today?"

"Mattie, you know we only do that on special occasions. Today is just a normal day."

For once he didn't argue, but his disappointment was clearly etched on his beautiful face. But it hadn't been a normal week, and Angela wasn't sure when it would be 'normal' again.

"Okay Mattie; change of mind. Let's do it. Only this once, mind."

"Yay! Love ya Mum."

"Love you too, Mattie—and not just for hamburgers!"

Twenty minutes later, they sat on a bench outside the hamburger joint. Angela wiped the dribbles from her chin. Eating hamburgers elegantly was impossible.

"Mum—how do you know they won't come back?"

There was no need to ask who he was talking about. "I told you yesterday, Mattie. We found who they were and they've been dealt with. They definitely won't be bothering us again."

"But why did they come in the first place?"

What to say? She should have thought more about this. "They were looking for someone else, someone I know. They thought I could help them find this person. They realise now it was the wrong thing to do and they've changed their minds. They won't do it again."

"That's good. I didn't like them frightening Nan like that." He took another mouthful of his hamburger.

"Mattie, best you don't tell anyone about this. It's a family secret."

"Luke knows. He's not family."

"No, he's not, but Luke helped us. He won't tell anyone, and nor will Jimmy. We don't want to upset other people. We'll just keep it between us. You can say we stayed with a friend for a couple of days but that's all."

If Mattie was stewing, perhaps her mother was as well. It prompted Angela to ring Louise after they returned home.

"Hi Mum. Just wanted to check you slept okay. No bumps in the night or anything like that."

"No dear, I'm fine. It was an adventure, one I could have done without, but what's life without a little excitement? I made a new friend in Maria, so something good came out of the experience."

"Glad to hear it. I'm just so sorry you got caught up in it all. Perhaps I could take the car out for a run tomorrow, and we could go for a drive. What about a country trip? It might be a nice break and change of scene. We could have lunch at a country pub."

"If you're serious about that, there's a quilting exhibition in Mt Hawthorn, and I'd love to see that. There are interesting curio shops in the village and some great cafés as well. You won't have to twist my arm."

They finalised details and Angela reviewed her to-do list for the weekend. To be doing the washing and planning the shopping list seemed terribly mundane after the week they'd had, but as she told herself, *suck it up, sister.*

"Don't forget the pancakes, Mum," Mattie reminded.

"What about the pancakes? You must have eaten enough to last you for a month."

"But Maria said she was giving you her recipe." Mattie was not going to let her off this hook. "You promised you'd make some."

She had too. Angela added buttermilk to the list. She had everything else. It might not match up to the light and fluffy pancakes that they'd savoured in Maria's kitchen, and there was one essential ingredient she'd never be able to buy; Luke Johnson's presence in her life. She pushed the thought aside and continued with her chores.

The weather gods were smiling on them the next day. Angela and Mattie picked up Louise mid-morning, and headed towards the outer reaches of the city and the road that led to Mt Hawthorn. Angela took the scenic rather than the direct route, and they stopped at one point to buy some roadside produce from a local farmer. Mattie entertained himself by counting the number of black and white cows he could see, and Angela and Louise drowned out the counting with enthusiastic vocal renditions of the tracks played on the radio.

They arrived with enough time to visit the quilting exhibition in the local institute building and spent an hour admiring the beautiful craftwork before Mattie's patience ran out.

"Are we finished yet? I'm starving."

"No you're not, Mattie. You had a snack in the car. You can wait a little longer."

"But this is bo-o-oring. Isn't there anything else to look at?"

Louise and Angela exchanged a resigned glance. It wasn't the most entertaining exhibition for a small boy. They'd completed a circuit of the hall, and purchased a raffle ticket in support of the local hospital, so they headed back into the street in search of lunch. They had to choose between the cafés and a couple of pubs.

The courtyard of one of the pubs won the contest, and with another family there as well, Mattie soon made friends with another boy of similar age while they waited for their orders to arrive. Angela and the other mother exchanged knowing smiles as the boys sought each other out, and discussed the merits of the trading cards each had been collecting.

"Mattie seems to have recovered well from his experiences last week," Louise said. "He's a resilient child. You've done well, Angela."

"He is a good kid. Maria's cooking was a big hit. I don't think I'll ever live up to it. The Lego in his room was a big attraction as well. I wonder who normally occupies it."

"I can answer that. Maria told me about it over morning tea."

"Why am I not surprised? I should have realised you would have got all the goss. Who is the child and where is he now?" Angela didn't even attempt to hide her curiosity. Her mother wouldn't have been fooled anyway.

"He's Luke's nephew. Clara, Luke's sister, died of breast cancer and the child spent some time with Luke during the final stages of her illness and then in the aftermath. The boy has now moved interstate to live with his father. Luke was sad at the lost contact, though the offer exists for holidays, so his room remains as we found it."

"That's so sad. It makes you think, doesn't it? You never know what is around the corner. Speaking of which, I've been thinking about a business idea, Mum."

Louise raised questioning eyebrows, waiting for her daughter to elaborate.

"It's a bit different to bookkeeping. Hear me out. I'm thinking of buying a run-down beauty salon and giving it a makeover."

The eyebrows now expressed surprise. Angela took a breath and outlined her idea and the concepts behind it. Louise asked a few questions and pursed her lips as she considered what her daughter was proposing. "It's not what I would have expected you to suggest, but the idea has some merits. Have you sought advice from Sasha and Renato?"

"They've given me tentative support. Sasha introduced me to an industry contact and that has helped with my research. I know it's a risk, Mum but I'm ready for something different for a whole range of reasons."

Louise slowly nodded her head. "Your occupation has served you well so far, but in the circumstances, I think it's time for a change, don't you?"

Angela looked at her mother, searching for hidden meaning in those eyes. What did she know? Louise just smiled sweetly. It wasn't a question she could ask and anyway conversation was interrupted by the arrival of their meals. As she called Mattie to come and get his lunch, Angela was reminded of Sasha's comment. *Never underestimate your mother*.

Whatever her decisions, to an extent it had to be business as usual. That meant her sessions with Mr Monday and Mr Tuesday went ahead as planned. As far as those gentlemen were concerned, there was no disruption to arrangements.

Angela still went to the apartment on other days of the week. It was her place of work, and where she preferred to study and undertake any research. There was no risk of being lured aside by domestic detritus. She drove herself for a change, not feeling that Jimmy was needed on a day like this.

The ring tone on the work phone on the second Wednesday of her new arrangement was unexpected. Not many people had that number.

"Hello?"

"Angelique? It's Stephen. I wanted to thank you properly for what you did. With all the excitement the other week, I didn't do that."

"That's okay, Stephen but thank you for calling." Angela had assumed she wouldn't hear from him again—not on this number, anyway.

"Will you join me for lunch today? I can send a car for you."

This could get complicated. "It's kind of you, Stephen, but not necessary. I'm just pleased we found out who was behind it and the fact no-one was hurt."

"As I was the main object of David Cornell's attentions I'm really happy about that too. Still, let me send the car for you. I know it's not Friday, but something you said that day got me thinking and I'd like to discuss a proposition with you."

"Stephen, establishing a permanent one-on-one relationship simply isn't possible." She couldn't allow him to pursue that idea.

"Nice thought, enticing even, but that wasn't what I was proposing. Meet me for lunch and I'll explain it to you. Pick you up at twelve?"

"Well…" She stood up and drifted towards the window, considering the request. *I'm not sure…. do I really need any more drama? Okay, I'm curious about what he has up his sleeve. Stephen's trustworthy; it's not as if he's going to sell me off to the slave-traders. Lunch could be nice.*

"… all right. I'm at the apartment. You have the address," she added, not hiding the ironic tone. "Call me when you're outside, and I'll come down."

Angela saved the file she'd been working on and shut down the laptop. She was intrigued. Who wouldn't be? Under current circumstances she had to think a little more broadly but if Stephen thought he could set up his own 'coaching establishment' with her running the show, he had another think coming.

What to wear? The leather and leopard skin combo she'd worn on their last intimate assignation was not appropriate. If Stephen had a proposition to put to her, then it had to be about business. Surveying the wardrobe she kept in the apartment, she selected a suit that best conveyed a this-is-professional-don't-mess-with-me image. She swept her hair up into a sleek chignon, and placed pearl earrings in her ears. A twirl before the mirror confirmed she had the right image.

When Stephen messaged her to indicate the car was approaching, she took the elevator downstairs to meet it. Mixed emotions swirled. There was curiosity about what he might suggest, combined with concern this was something she was going to regret.

Angela paused to ensure it was the right car before pressing the security button opening the doors to the building. Jimmy's training rang in her hears. 'Check, double check, and then check again.' Before coming down to the foyer, she had sent him a quick text message saying where she was going and why. In the circumstances, she couldn't be too careful.

The car pulled under the portico, and the driver got out and opened the rear door. She could see Stephen seated in the back. No sign of anything untoward. She pressed the button and stepped into the late morning sunshine.

"Angelique—how good to see you." Stephen kissed her cheek as she slid onto the seat beside him. "Thank you for coming. You look magnificent, as always."

"Thank you, Stephen. You seem to have recovered from the adventures of the other week." She checked that the privacy screen between them and the driver was in place.

156

"I'm keen to hear what you have in mind. Where are we going, by the way?"

"To answer your second question, we're lunching in one of the restaurants at Casino Royale. It's owned by Lundy Holdings, as I'm sure you know. One thing you can be sure of—it's going to be great service."

He gave a boyish, almost gleeful grin. "As for the proposal, all in good time. I want you to see the place first."

So it had something to do with the casino. Her feeling of unease heightened.

They pulled into a secure car park and stepped into a private elevator, taking them to one of the upper floors. Stepping out, Angela saw they were in the foyer area to a restaurant. Not just any restaurant. The thickness of the carpet and the furnishings ensured it was quiet, and exuded an air of luxurious opulence.

"Mr Lundy, let me take your jacket. Your table is ready." One of the staff took the jacket and gestured towards a table on the far side of the room. It was by the window, and had a fabulous view, partially over the city and partially over the bay.

Stephen took her elbow and guided her in that direction. "This way. We should be able to chat undisturbed over here."

Service was efficient and unobtrusive. With relatively little fuss, food and wine was ordered and promptly delivered. Their conversation covered general topics while people were coming and going. By the time they were left alone, they had exhausted the weather and a discussion of the latest shows in town.

"So, Stephen, you didn't just bring me here to experience a wonderful dining experience. Why don't you tell me what you have in mind?" Angela waited while he blotted his mouth on the napkin and sat back in his chair.

"Firstly, I have to thank you for your assistance last week. It was a situation with the potential to end very differently than it did, and I suspect it would have been to the detriment of all concerned. The fact that it didn't was due significantly to you. I appreciate that."

"I won't belittle the situation by saying 'It was nothing', but I'm also relieved we were able to contain the drama. It wasn't just me, you know. Luke Johnson and Jimmy played major roles in protecting you. Have you spoken to your mother?"

"I have. Not an easy conversation, as I was still angry at Cornell, but that's not the fault of his wife and daughter. It's them I feel sorry for. I convinced my mother that theirs was a justifiable cause, but it's not only up to her. She's taking it back to the assessment panel. I'll let you know when I hear the result. Should be soon."

They were drinking a sparkling pinot noir, and Stephen topped up their glasses before picking up his and raising it in salute.

"Angelique, you know casino operations come under my control, both in Australia as well as overseas. It's an important part of Lundy Holdings. There are two aspects of casino operations. There's the public side, with which you may already be familiar. That's open to anyone, provided they satisfy the requirements of security who monitor our guests."

He paused, taking a sip of his wine and gestured towards the windows. "Fabulous view, isn't it? There are many features of the casino that are different on this level."

He turned back to look at her. "This is where we cater for our more discerning clients. We ensure discretion and privacy. Some of them fly into the country in private aircraft and are transferred directly to this establishment. They fly in below the radar, so to speak."

He sat forward and his voice dropped a level. "They come directly to this floor, and here we provide private gaming rooms, fine dining and the sort of accommodation they and their entourage would expect."

He paused for effect. "We ensure their time at Casino Royale is first class. There is a lot of work and expertise that goes into ensuring their experience here is unparalleled in every way."

"That's fascinating, Stephen, but what is it to do with me? If you think I'm providing executive coaching services to your fly-in-fly-out clients, you've wasted both your and my time." A flush of annoyance rose from her neckline. The feeling of disbelief clenched her innards. He reached out to take her hand, shaking his head.

"Angelique, I would never be so crass. That's not my intention at all. I've learned enough about you to know that you're a first-class operator. You're discreet, sophisticated and have a level head. Those are all valuable attributes."

He topped up her wine glass. "I want you to run the Presidential level operations."

10 – A Job Offer

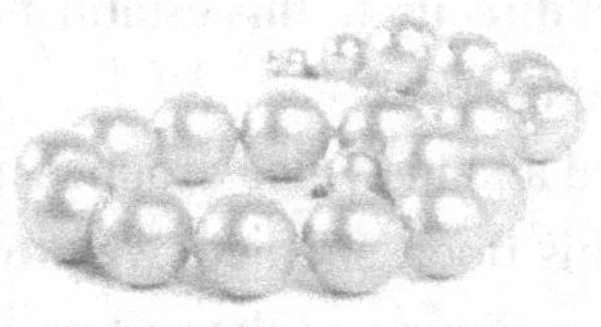

"Me? I don't know anything about running a casino."

"You don't have to. I employ people with expertise in that area. I'm not intimately involved with this side of things but have qualified staff for management operations. They are professionals in everything they do."

"That I can believe, if the business pages of the local paper are accurate. It seems you've had a record year."

She'd done other research but that was a more clandestine activity, not to be disclosed. She'd even had debates with herself about her investment strategy. From a hard-nosed and rational perspective, purchasing shares in Lundy Holdings was probably a smart move. On the other hand, did she want to invest in a company that made its fortune at the expense of others? It was a moot point, given it was the source of income from which Stephen paid for executive coaching.

"It's been a very good year," he agreed. "One indicator is the activity on the Presidential level. These clients are not your ordinary punters. These are people of substantial means and who are used to the very best in life. They are also huge gamblers. Their value to the business is significant. It's in our interest to look after them, and that's where you come in."

Angela stiffened. She stared at him, waiting for what was to come next. She gripped the stem of her wine glass, fearful of what it might be. He leaned forward a grin. She almost expected him to wriggle in his seat with excitement,

"Angelique, I want you to oversee the operations on the Presidential level. Those clients are important, and they must be kept happy. Your role would be that of a hostess if you like, ensuring any special requirements are met and that their experience within the casino exceeds their expectations."

Having delivered what he clearly thought was an irresistible offer, he sat back again. "I've known for a while that we needed someone in that role but hadn't followed up on it. Last night, it suddenly hit me. You'd be perfect."

He punctuated this statement with a finger stabbed in her direction.

Don't point at me like that. "Stephen, I need clarity on what you mean by special requirements."

"No, Angelique; absolutely not. I am not expecting you to meet *that* sort of requirement. This is strictly out of the boudoir." He hesitated, his face doing contortions of anguish. "Of course, there may be requests for services of a personal nature, but there are agencies working in that arena. It's not something I promote or encourage. I wouldn't expect you to be involved in that."

"Don't you already have people doing this sort of work for you? People with prior experience and who know the industry?"

"It's not just experience that counts. There's a certain quality that's needed to succeed in this type of role. It doesn't hurt of course that you're exceptionally easy on the eye, and these high rolling clients, who are predominantly male, will appreciate that. They can be challenging in different situations. I've already seen how you can handle yourself. After what you've been through, this will be a breeze."

Her eyebrows arched in disbelief. "Thanks for the vote of confidence, but I have my own plans to consider. As you have assumed, the events of the last week have had a negative impact on my operations and therefore my income, but I was already exploring options for a new business, something quite unrelated."

His face dropped. "Won't you at least consider it? The salary will be worth it, I promise. You don't have to decide immediately." The boyish grin was back. "Tomorrow will be fine."

The waiter appeared to replenish their water, and to enquire if they needed anything. At the brief shake of Stephen's head, the man quietly withdrew. Angela waited until she could speak privately again. Her mind was racing. Could this be the stop-gap she needed, something to tide her over until she could launch the salon business?

"I appreciate the offer, Stephen, I really do—"

"I can hear the 'but' coming," he interrupted. "Don't turn me down yet. You can make good money here. You've got your son to think of after all."

162

He noted her look of concern. "I saw him at Luke Johnson's place last week," he said. "Looking at him, I would have guessed he was your child, even if I didn't hear him call you *Mum*."

She'd tried to make sure Mattie was out of the way. She hadn't realised Stephen had seen him. Life was becoming ever more complicated.

"You'll understand then, Stephen, that all decisions I make are with reference to my son's welfare as well. Flexibility is crucial, and because of limitations in my current line of work, my plans involve developing a different business model that will allow me to have more time available for Mattie."

She poured herself a glass of water. The wine with lunch had left her feeling dehydrated. It also gave her time to think. Sort of. She wasn't sure what to make of it all.

"Why aren't you starting this new business now? Can you tell me about it?" Stephen looked genuinely interested.

"I'm not ready to talk about it yet. I'm still in the research phase. It's a mainstream occupation, and will allow me to structure my life around Mattie's needs. As to why I haven't started it, that's simple. In part, I haven't completed the research but the major factor is sorting out the finances. I need a certain level of capital to support this venture. I was expecting to provide my coaching services for a while yet. Last week put paid to that."

He sat pondering, his chin resting on the steeple of his hands. His eyes bored into her. Angela could almost see the cogs turning. What was he thinking?

"This might suit you for the interim. It would help you achieve a more solid financial footing, and would give me time to find someone equally as good as you. It's the least I can do for you. Of course, you may find you love it so much you decide to stay."

"I can't work the sort of hours you keep. As you have noticed, I have a child. I'm a working mother."

"As far as hours go, it would be flexible. Sometimes we would have high profile, high needs guests accommodated here, and then you would have to be on-call from early in the day. Other times, the pressure would be late afternoon or even in the evenings. When things are quiet, you could disappear, work on your business idea, whatever. It would be up to you."

She broke off eye contact, looking instead towards the view. Outside was a scene of picturesque normality, but inside she was in turmoil. She shook her head at the incongruity.

Stephen directed puppy-dog eyes towards her. "I can make a suite available to you for your use when you're working. Your son could stay there as well, on the proviso of course that he never came anywhere near the clients and the gaming rooms. There are strict laws about minors in casinos."

Mattie in a place like this? He must be joking. She looked around her. It was a rarefied atmosphere, not the place for a child at all. It simply was not possible.

"You'd receive an appropriate salary of course," Stephen added.

He went on to name a figure that left her speechless. She didn't know ordinary people earned money like that. Not unless they were providing superior executive coaching services. Could she do it? How would that work? What would she tell her mother? What about Mr. Monday and Mr. Tuesday? The decisions were overwhelming. With money like that, she would make the final payments on the apartment quicker than anticipated. The salon would become a reality sooner rather than later. She couldn't dismiss it out of hand.

"Stephen, what you're proposing needs careful consideration. Do you mind if I get back to you on this?"

"Like I said, tomorrow is fine."

"Oh, so no pressure then? Perhaps. I'll give you a decision when I've made it. That's the best I can promise. Could we leave now? I've a few things to think about."

"Sure. I'll call for the car. I look forward to hearing from you."

"Sasha, it was a totally crazy offer. More than I currently earn, or rather, more than I did. I just don't know what to do."

After she was delivered back to the apartment, Angela collected her laptop and dropped in on her mentor. Normally, she would never do this unannounced but she desperately needed advice.

165

"Well, sit down and we'll have a cup of tea, or do you need coffee? Start at the beginning. Why did he make this offer?"

For once, they sat in the kitchen. When others weren't around, Sasha and Renato were less formal. While Sasha sat down at the table with her, Renato busied himself with the makings of the tea, and put out a plate of almond bread, made according to his mama's recipe.

"This man is full of surprises," Renato called over his shoulder. "After the shenanigans of last week, I thought you were not so impressed with him."

Angela took a deep breath and exhaled before replying, her face scrunched in reflection. "I've always liked Stephen. He's been a good client and ours has been a beneficial relationship. I was surprised by the petulance he displayed last week, but he was under a bit of pressure. For a couple of days, we had no idea what or who was behind the threats and the danger was very real. Don't forget, he doesn't know David Cornell as well as I do. His reaction wasn't unreasonable under the circumstances."

"True. None of us know how we would react until wearing those shoes," said Renato, bringing the cups to the table.

Angela outlined the proposal as she understood it, finishing with the salary offered and the hours Stephen had outlined.

Sasha's eyebrows raised in response to the figure mentioned. "That is indeed very generous. Astonishingly so. You have to think carefully about this. It may be the short term solution you need."

"But what about Mr. Monday and Mr. Tuesday? I couldn't continue to provide services to them."

"No, you couldn't. You were planning to make changes to your business activities anyway. So what's the problem?"

She needed to put all the objections on the table. Only then could she rationally consider the issues. "But Mattie—he needs me. This job has irregular hours and I would have to manage that somehow."

"Many parents have irregular hours, Angela. Think about nurses, or those in the police force for instance. At least you have your mother to help out and on those times when she is not available, you could afford to pay for an au pair." Sasha was using her best no-nonsense voice. She had a point.

"I'll speak to my mother. She needs to be on-board also. I already rely on her such a lot and this just adds to that situation."

"Good idea. Now what are you doing about the salon concept?"

"I haven't had time to think about it. All I've done is throw around names, trying to come up with something that has a bit of cachet. Angela's Beauty Salon doesn't do it for me."

There was a silence as they all contemplated the options. They tested each name, turning over the sounds and the images it conjured.

"Tres Chic?"

"No, sounds like a dress shop."

"About Face?"

"Nope. Already taken."

"Maison Angelique?"

Two pairs of eyes swivelled towards Angela.

"Sasha, I think that's it. It's so simple and obvious. Thank you so much—I'll register the name tomorrow. Now it's starting to seem real."

Her mood had lifted considerably by the time she walked through the front door. She was more-or-less resolved to taking the job with Stephen. It would only be short term and would be a means to an end. She had to keep that goal in sight.

The conversation with her mother came while Mattie was in the bath.

"But what exactly will you be doing," Louise asked, "and why has he offered you the job?"

Angela picked her words carefully. "He was impressed with how I handled David Cornell, and coupled with what he already knew of me, thought I would have the right attributes for the role."

She kicked off her shoes and massaged the balls of her feet. Would she have to wear killer shoes all the time? One more thing to consider. "It's just short term, Mum, until I can finance the salon. The salary's too good to refuse. The catch is the hours. It means I'll need more help with Mattie, but I'll be able to pay for that. I'm thinking of getting an au pair, someone who'll be available to look after him when I can't be here."

"I can do that, Angela. I don't like the idea of a stranger caring for him."

"But Mum, that's a huge imposition on you. You do so much for us already and you have your own life to live as well."

"I'll have plenty of time when Mattie's at school. As you say, it's only for a while. I can just sleep over here when you're working at night. If you're going to pay anyone, you can pay me."

There wasn't much Angela could say against that. Of course it would be preferable that her mother was looking after Mattie. It seemed there was no reason not to take the job. Decision made. She would call Stephen in the morning to tell him she would start the following week. She also needed to call Mr Monday and Mr Tuesday to cancel their appointments. It was the end of an era.

~

Luke looked at his watch and did some quick calculations. If he rang now, it might not be too late back in Melbourne. He hesitated, not sure whether to make the call or not. He wanted to know if there had been any consequences from the kidnap attempt.

Did he really need to know? Did he want to get that deeply involved? *Not really. I just want to hear her voice.* It would be weeks before he was back in Australia. That was too long to wait. He reached for his phone, only to be interrupted by a meeting delegate.

"There you are, Mr Johnson. Before we start the next session, there are some questions I'd like to ask you about quality assurance and maintenance."

"Sure. What would you like to know?" Luke put on his most attentive expression and talked the man through the issues. "I'm happy to do a site visit," he said. "Then we can look at the optimal solutions for your situation."

By the time he'd pleaded the need to use the bathroom and escaped, there were only a few minutes left before the meeting was due to start. That added the pressure he needed. Positioned behind a huge potted fern in the foyer area of the hotel, he quickly put through the call.

~

She was already in bed when she heard the ring tone for her private work phone. She wasn't asleep. The events of the day still played on her mind. She checked the caller ID. It was Luke Johnson.

"Luke… I wasn't expecting you to call. I thought you were out of the country." She held the quick surge of excitement in check so her voice sounded normal.

"I am. I'm in between meetings at the moment. I'm involved in back-to-back discussions, but you don't want to hear about that." *Yes I do. I want to hear about all of it. I especially want to hear you're working hard, and not wining and dining some other woman. Tell me more.*

"Don't work too hard." Her laugh sounded brittle.

"What else is there for me to do, seeing as you refused an offer to accompany me? I hope it's not too late for you?" His voice was low and teasing, with just a hint of reproach. It was a soft purring in her ear.

She settled back on the pillow as she listened to him, imagining how it would be if he were with her now. Her hand wandered down towards her centre of pleasure, and the nub already pulsating with desire.

"Not at all," she said huskily. "I'm already in bed, but still awake."

"Oh no," he groaned, "With that image in my mind, I won't be able to focus on this next meeting. I'll be thinking of being there with you. Tell me you're not wearing anything except those fabulous earrings of yours."

She laughed, surprised he'd remembered that comment. Was it only a couple of weeks ago? So much had happened since then.

Her mind wandered back to the last occasion he'd crept between her sheets, and more besides. Just the memory was enough to engulf her in a tidal flush. She breathed out slowly to refocus.

"I wondered if there was any fallout from recent events," he said. "How's Mattie? No nightmares or anything like that?"

"Not at all. He can't stop talking about our stay at your home. I'm not sure what held the greater attraction—Maria's pancakes or the box of Lego in the room he used." She paused, pushing her hair back from her face. "Luke… I heard about your sister. Her loss must have been devastating."

"It was. It was a while ago now, although occasionally I'm caught by unexpected memories. Both our parents had already died, so we were close. Her son, Peter, stayed with me sometimes. I don't see much of him anymore."

He cleared his throat. "I didn't mean to sound such a sad-sack. That wasn't why I rang. Changing the subject, has Lundy come good with any funding in support of Melanie's expenses in the States?"

"I raised the issue with him today, actually. The details have been forwarded to his mother's foundation, so now it's just a waiting game."

"He hasn't stuck his hand in his own pocket then? I thought his day was Friday?"

Something told her to keep quiet about the offer. She tensed at the sudden abruptness of his tone. "It was a follow-up meeting, not coaching. Stephen wanted to express his thanks for helping out last week. I imagine he still needs time to process everything that happened and to deal with his anger at David Cornell. That's not unreasonable."

There was a strained silence before Luke commented again. "I suppose some people need time to man up."

She had expected more tolerance. He wasn't the one who had been threatened. "Was there anything else, Luke?"

"No, not really—well yes, but doesn't matter. I'm sorry I disturbed you. Sleep well."

He disconnected the call. There was a tightness in her chest and an ache in her head. Life could be complicated. She lay back on the pillows and turned out the bedside lamp. Sleep did not come easy.

~

Negotiations with Stephen were completed to her satisfaction. It was agreed the position was short term, but that Angela would give two-week's notice of when she intended leaving. She would also be provided with a suite at the casino on the Presidential level for her use. She would make herself available according to demand and sometimes that would mean staying overnight. When activity on the Presidential level was slow, she was free to take that time off.

172

It would give her time to work on the business, or complete the outstanding finance modules in her studies. It was a time of transition and it was exciting.

"Angelique, if you need anything, give me a call. You've got my number"

She was more nervous than she expected on her first day. Stephen took her to the HR Department to fill in the appropriate forms and to collect her staff pass.

"I feel like the new kid at school," she confided. "Everyone must be wondering how I got the job given I've not worked in this industry before.

"You got the job because you're the best qualified, and because I decided and I'm the boss."

In his own environment, Stephen was more assured. It was a different side to the man she knew on Fridays. He introduced her to the key staff members and gave her a detailed tour of the Presidential floor, including the room allocated to her.

They got as far as the kitchen on that level, when his phone rang.

"Yes… but can't anyone else…?" He sighed with exasperation. "I'll be there soon."

Disconnecting the call, he turned to Angela. "Sorry, an issue has arisen back in the office. I'll have to leave you to it. I'll catch up with you later."

Angela wandered back to the Presidential reception area. She had been allocated a small office, and in the absence of anything else to do, adjusted the chair height and sat at the desk. Self-doubt engulfed her. How long could she hide in here? What was she really supposed to be doing?

The door flew open and Celia, the receptionist stood there. "You'd better come quickly. He's on the balcony."

"Who is? What's the matter?"

"It's Mr. Yamamoto. He's climbed up onto the parapet of the balcony. He's says he's going to jump."

"Oh no, not today!" She hurried after the woman who gave her an odd look.

"What's today got to do with it?"

"Nothing, I wasn't expecting something like this, that's all."

They hurried down the passage, Celia leading the way to the man's suite. A staff member was standing in the doorway to the balcony, pleading with the man who was balanced on the parapet, still holding onto the wall beside him. Glancing around as they entered the room, the steward stepped back, allowing Angela to take his place.

She exchanged a stricken glance with Celia. "I can't do this," she mouthed. Celia nodded her head emphatically, pointing to Angela and then back to Mr. Yamamoto. Angela rolled her eyes and stepped forward. Her first day and she was already responsible for the life of a guest.

"Mr. Yamamoto—I'm Angela Benson, the hostess on this floor. This is my first day working on the Presidential level. I'm here to be of service to our guests, but I'm still learning how to do that. Please tell me how I might help you today."

She was surprised to see how young he was. His figure was so slight a puff of wind could blow him over the edge if he didn't hang on tightly. As it was, the breeze ruffled the legs of his trousers. The rise and fall of his chest was the only visible movement as he stared straight ahead.

Don't look down; please don't look down.

The young man didn't look at her. "Go away."

"I can't do that, Mr. Yamamoto. If my job is to help you, I have to stay here until you tell me how I can do that."

"You can't help me. Go away."

How was she supposed to handle this? Angela took a surreptitious step closer, not taking her eyes off the man. "Are you alone? Is there someone you would like me to call?"

"No person. Go, please."

"Mr, Yamamoto, I need this job. I can't get the sack over this and if you jump off this balcony, that's what will happen. I will lose my job and won't be able to look after my little boy."

"Not my problem."

"Well, what *is* your problem? Please tell me." She took another step closer and reached out to grasp the back of a chair that was on the balcony. "Do you mind if I sit down? My shoes are killing me."

For the first time, he glanced in her direction, looking down at her feet before looking away again. At least he was connecting with her on some level.

Her lips felt dry. She tried not to lick them. She slipped her shoes off. If she had to make a sudden lunge for him, it would be easier to move quickly without them.

"Tell me," she repeated. "What's making you feel you have to do this?"

"No money. Lost all the money. Shame on my family."

"I'm sorry to hear that, Mr. Yamamoto. Won't your death bring even greater shame on your family? Won't they be upset you didn't trust them enough to talk to them?"

"You don't know my family."

"No, I don't, but I'm a mother. I know how I would feel if something happened to my son, no matter what the circumstances. Don't do this to your mother. It will break her heart. She will never recover." For a heartbreaking moment, she imagined how she would feel if this were Mattie standing on the edge.

From her vantage point, she got a glimpse of a tear, which hovered on the brink for a moment before sliding down his face. She held her breath. This was a deciding moment. He would either step forward into messy oblivion, or climb down from the wall.

She reached out her hand. "Take my hand, Mr. Yamamoto and I'll help you down. Sit down with me and tell me about your mother."

It was a long moment before he turned his head and looked directly at her. She could see now that tears were coursing freely down his face. He looked to her hand. She forced her lips into a semblance of a smile. After another hesitation, he reached out and took her hand, using it for support as he jumped off the wall. The crisis was averted.

Angela hadn't realised that others had collected in the room behind her during the drama, but they now moved forward and ushered Mr. Yamamoto back into the room. Celia threw an arm around Angela's shoulders.

"You were amazing. You knew just what to say. Pick up your shoes – I think we should move back inside and lock this door."

Letting out a pent-up breath, Angela slipped her shoes back on and followed the group leading the distressed man to safety. Celia said he would be relocated to a room without a balcony, and a doctor would be summoned to assess his mental health.

Conscious of her promise to him, Angela sat with the man for a while and listened to his story. He confessed he'd been carried away, swayed by the luxurious surroundings and the influence of other players at the poker table. He would normally stop at a given point decided in advance, but this time, buoyed by his success, he had raised the stakes and lost it all. He was embarrassed and knowing how disappointed his father would be, felt he had no option other than to end it all.

Angela was glad when the psychologist on call to the casino came to take over. She felt so sad for the young man. Thank goodness, the lure of the wheel or the cards held no attraction for her.

11 – Life in a Casino

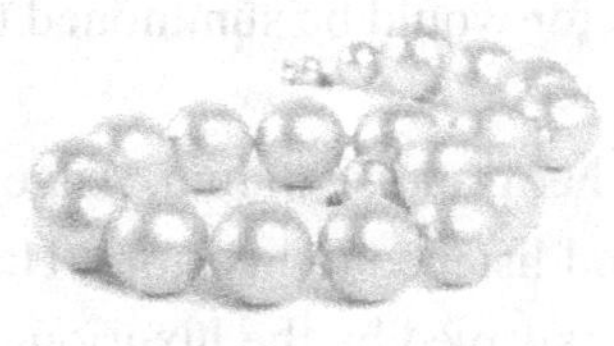

Once Angela recovered from the emotional fall-out associated with Mr. Yamamoto's suicide attempt, she felt she could handle anything.

"We don't get many jumpers," Celia cheerfully informed her. "They're the easy ones, really. They're waiting for someone to talk them out of it."

"You mean, I could have just said 'Now don't be silly; get down from there' and he would have meekly complied?"

"Well, perhaps not that easily. You did really well, by the way. It's the ones who hide away quietly in their rooms you have to worry about."

"I'll keep an eye on them," Angela said, not really sure how she was going to do that. Perhaps she should request regular reports on those who had experienced big losses.

Stephen was equally enthusiastic. "I knew I'd done the right thing in hiring you. You were brilliant. The Yamamotos are a very important family. I hate to think what the fall-out would have been if he'd jumped. His father would never have forgiven me."

"Surely the greater impact would have been the death of that young man," Angela reminded him.

"Yes, of course. Absolutely."

Angela could only shake her head at the world in which she found herself, and the attitudes of those who lived in it.

During the next week, she didn't see much of Stephen, as he wasn't involved in daily operations but when he was in the building, he sought her out. She was wary, always expecting he might put the hard word on her, or suggest that their coaching relationship resume.

"Staff treating you well?" he asked as they took lunch in the dining room at the beginning of her second week.

She nodded. "They've been such a help, mentoring me through a huge learning curve. I'm very grateful."

"I'm pleased you settled in so well." He looked at her intently. "I still have the regular Friday appointment blanked out in my calendar." He hesitated. "Perhaps now that the drama is over, we could resume that booking?"

"You know better than to ask. We've moved on from there but if you still require executive coaching, I'm sure I can provide some suitable referrals."

"It wouldn't be the same without you." He wore his best soulful expression.

Angela was not in the least impressed. She was reminded of little boys who've been denied a treat. Time to change the subject. "Any news from your Mother's foundation? Are they going to support Melanie Cornell?"

"It's not the usual cause they take up, but because I specifically asked, it's been put on the agenda. They meet monthly, and should be convening later in the week. I'll let you know as soon as I hear."

Angela picked her words carefully. "You know, Stephen, if you can afford executive coaching, you can probably afford to contribute to this trip to the States."

"Support David Cornell? Why should I do that? He's the one who put his family in this situation to say nothing of what he intended for me."

Angela regarded him silently. She wasn't impressed, even if it was an understandable response.

"What?" he demanded. "What are you expecting of me?"

"Compassion, Stephen. Compassion for a mother and daughter who are suffering life-shattering consequences due to a situation that is not of their making."

"You know how to pull the heartstrings, don't you?" He pulled a wry face as he selected and broke open a roll from the bread basket and slathered it in butter. "I tell you what—if the foundation awards the Cornells a grant, I'll top it up."

"Very generous of you." Angela smiled sweetly. "And if the grant isn't approved? What then?"

His sigh was theatrical. "You're like a terrier with a bone. I'll think about it, okay? No promises."

Angela knew enough not to push it.

Managing guest relationships could also be tricky. One particular gentleman, who regularly flew in from Singapore, thought Angela might be a side benefit to his premium status.

"You are a very beautiful woman."

"Thank you. I hope your stay here has been enjoyable, Mr. Chan."

"If you come to my room this evening, it will be worth your while. I am a very rich man, and Lady Luck has smiled on me during this visit."

"That will not be possible, Mr. Chan. My duties do not extend to providing room service."

"I can buy you anything you want: dresses; jewellery? You tell me."

"I don't need your jewellery, Mr. Chan; I'm not for sale. Please let reception know if there is anything else we can help you with."

She smiled sweetly as she took her leave, determined more than ever to pursue her dream. It was the incident with Mr. Chan that made her review her future plans, and what she might do to take a step in that direction.

Pulling into the driveway that evening, she was exhausted. Earlier in the day, one guest appeared to be having a heart attack, but fortunately it was only a panic attack. It was panic all round for a while, until the resident medical officer attended and diagnosed the problem.

Another, who had achieved greater success than Mr. Yamamoto, requested she accompany him to Tiffany's, where he selected a bracelet for his wife. He wanted a woman's advice on the purchase. Angela felt faint when she saw the price tag, and was firm in her refusal when he wanted to buy a slightly cheaper bracelet for her also as a thank-you gift.

Louise Benson was still on child care duty. She often stayed over, as she was doing this particular evening. After greeting her mother , Angela slipped upstairs to check on her son in the bath. He was often asleep before she finished up at work.

"Hey, Mattie, how was your day?"

"Mum! I didn't hear you come in."

"I'm not surprised. You were making enough racket up here to be heard all the way down the street. Where did all that water come from?" she said in mock horror, surveying the mess on the floor.

"Sorry, Mum. I was practising my swimming."

"In the bath? I think there's more water on the floor than in the tub. If you hop out now, I'll be able to read you a story before it's sleep time."

"Yay! I'll pick the story."

By the time she came back downstairs, Angela was more than ready to share a glass of wine with her mother.

"Honestly mum, some people have no idea on the value of money. It's easy come, easy go."

The older woman shook her head in amazement at the revelations. "Just keep focussed on the end goal. It's helping you get there quicker than you anticipated."

"I think about that every day. With that in mind, I've joined the Institute of Beauty Management. I want to establish my industry networks."

"Great idea. Learn as much as you can. I'm expecting platinum customer service, you know." She busied herself with serving up the evening meal, as she recounted the events of the day. "Incidentally, I met Maria for coffee. She kept telling me how much she enjoyed having everyone there for those couple of days. I think she gets a bit lonely, especially now Luke is overseas."

"She must rattle around in that big house on her own," Angela agreed. "Aren't there any other support staff?"

"It seems not. Jimmy has dropped in a couple of times though."

Angela couldn't hide her surprise. She still felt guilty about Jimmy. In taking the role at the Casino, she didn't need his services any more. She drove her own car to work and a secure car park was provided. Casino security staff were available to take care of any unpleasantness.

"Was he looking for more of Maria's cooking? That wouldn't surprise me."

Louise laughed. "He may have been, but knowing Luke Johnson was away, he just wanted to check on the place. He was making sure Maria was fine, that nobody was watching the house, and of course, that the magnificent collection of cars was secure."

"Ah—now we're getting to the crux of the matter."

Knowing Jimmy as she did, it wouldn't only be the cars. He would feel a sense of responsibility to Maria, given that Luke was not around. He would want to check that the men engaged by David Cornell were not going to cause trouble.

It gave her an idea. Perhaps Luke needed someone to look after the cars and general security. Should she call him? It would give her a valid excuse to do so. She didn't know exactly when he was returning to Australia, nor when she would see him again. Without the coaching, there wasn't a reason to do so. Their last conversation had been a bit tense and this would be a legitimate excuse to contact him again.

She waited until later in the evening, when Mattie was asleep and Louise was watching television. Retreating to her room, she took out her phone but hesitated. She hadn't felt like this since she was an anxious teenager. Perhaps he would be in a meeting. Perhaps the call would be inconvenient. On the other hand, he didn't have to answer it. If he didn't want to take it, he could just let the call go through to voicemail. She dialled his number.

The phone rang for an indeterminate time. She was about to disconnect, when it was answered and Luke was there.

"Hello? Angelique? This is an unexpected delight. Is everything all right?"

The pulse in her throat gave a jump at the sound of his voice. "Everything's fine," she said. *Except for my heart, which is dancing a tango.* "I have a suggestion to put to you."

"I'm all ears," he said, "but if you're thinking of joining me now, it's a bit late. I expect to be home by the end of next week."

"I'm calling about Jimmy, actually."

"You want Jimmy to join me? I thought you would have picked up by now that I don't swing that way."

She rolled her eyes, even though the effect was wasted on him. "I no longer employ Jimmy as my driver and security consultant. I know he's kept an eye on Maria and your place in your absence. Have you thought about using him yourself in that capacity and to also look after your collection of cars?"

"Interesting idea. I like the guy. He's solid. It was good of him to drop in on her."

"He's considerate like that. Also, he probably couldn't bear the thought of anything happening to those cars. Surely you have a need for a consultant with his talents?"

"It must be important to you, for you to call me."

He would never know how important it had been just to hear his voice again.

"I didn't know when you were coming back, so wanted to put the suggestion to you now. That way, arrangements can be put in place."

"I'm not averse to the idea; it has definite possibilities. I'll think it over and have a chat to him."

"That's great. He's done so much for me; I feel a degree of responsibility for his future."

"So, if it's not too inquisitive, what are you doing now if you're not 'coaching'? Can I surmise you're reserving your services for me?"

"Now why would I do that?" Angela's voice dropped to a deeper, sexier register.

"I could think of a few reasons, but mainly because I've always had the impression you enjoyed it; because I think we have a connection that's worth fostering; and because after this length of time apart, I think it's going to be worth waiting for. Don't you?"

That was an understatement. What role would he have in her life on his return? Angela knew what she wanted if she was honest, but Luke was talking about sex—hot, passionate, pulsating sex. She bit her lip. Could Luke ever see her as Angela, and not Angelique?

"Are you still there?" Luke raised his voice.

"Yes, yes I'm still here. Sorry, I must have missed what you just said."

"I said, 'I'm looking forward to coming home.' Is there anything you would like me to bring back for you? A Persian rug perhaps, or exotic perfume from the Souk?"

The question conjured up exotic images of regret. She wished she'd been able to travel with him.

"I think surprises are best, don't you?" She still hadn't told him what she was doing. She had a feeling he wasn't going to like it. That was unfortunate, but it wasn't really anything to do with Luke. "To answer your earlier question, I have a short term role in Customer Service at the Casino, working for Stephen Lundy on the Presidential Floor."

"Why would you work for someone like him? What are you doing, or is that too personal a question?"

"There's no reason not to work for Stephen, and earning an income is a necessity for me. Recent events dictated a change in business activities and this is it—for now anyway while I put other plans in place. I have a specialist role, looking after the welfare of guests who are accommodated on this level."

"What does that mean exactly?"

"It means I ensure they enjoy their visit to Casino Royale, and if there are any problems I do what I can to solve them. Simple, really."

"I'll take your word for it. I don't know much about that world."

186

"Neither did I until recently" She slid back on the bed, arranging the pillows for support as she leant against the bedhead. "I hope your travels have been productive for your business." What she really wanted to say was '*Luke, just come home safely.*' That would be laying her feelings on the table.

"Sure. It's going to pay off. Look, I've got to go; I'm running late for the next meeting. I'll call you when I get back."

Then he was gone, and she was left, staring at her phone. He'd said they had a connection and he'd call her on his return. That was positive, surely? Her heart did a little flip.

Luke rubbed his eyes, trying to make sense of what Angelique had just told him. He was still conflicted about whether he was talking to Angela or Angelique. She'd only rung him on Jimmy's behalf, not because she wanted to speak to him. He was reasonably sure she only thought of him as a paying client, one whose concern didn't extend beyond the bedroom. His interest, as far as their physical relationship went was strong, and he made no apologies for that. He'd not met another woman who was able to evoke the response in him that she did.

It wasn't only that. He admired the strong feisty woman he'd got to know and then there was the other side of her; the caring mother and the daughter, who created a stable family life for both Mattie and Louise. Dammit, he was jealous. The business had been all consuming, and he'd done well but as

Maria frequently told him, his big house needed a family. To his mind, not just any family; only one that fitted in as naturally as they all had a couple of weeks ago.

He was uncomfortable about the fact she worked for Lundy, but it wasn't any of his business. He knew that. It was better than the executive coaching, but only just. Could they start on a new basis once he returned to Australia? All he could do was ask, and he was going to give it his best shot. There was still time to think about how and when.

The rest of the week was relatively uneventful. Angela felt at home in the casino environment now, and had fostered good working relationships with other employees. It was a change after working independently as she had in recent years. She even looked forward to some of the staff gossip and interaction. Celia could always be relied on to relay crucial information about the guests on their floor, and what was happening behind staff doors.

"Angela, Mr. Aboud is asking for you."

"Did he say what he wanted this time?"

Celia merely shrugged. "I didn't ask. He always wants to know if you're on duty. I think you've won a heart."

Angela suppressed a sigh and composed her expression before leaving her office to meet him. He was seated in a large armchair in the reception area, and levered himself out as she approached. A man of substantial girth, he was expensively dressed and there was a sweet, cloying scent that lingered in his proximity.

188

"Mr. Aboud—I hope you've had a successful afternoon at the tables."

"Indeed, Miss Angela, I am very happy with events of today. I would be even happier if you would join me for dinner this evening. I am dining in the restaurant, and it will be very sad if I am forced to eat alone."

"Surely there are some of your fellow travellers who would like to join you?"

"I can dine with them anytime. I don't have to travel to Australia for that. Here, I prefer the company of a beautiful woman."

He travelled with an entourage, but they were nowhere in sight. Perhaps they were still trying their luck. His family had a major jewellery empire, and he was an important client, as Stephen had mentioned a couple of times. That knowledge played heavily on her mind as she considered her options. She couldn't really refuse. She agreed to meet him in the dining room at seven, and rang her mother to say she wouldn't be home until late.

"Kiss Mattie good night for me," she said, with an ache in her heart. She missed that ritual with her boy. Retreating to the room allocated to her, she changed into evening clothes. Dress standards were required of guests in the restaurant, and she followed the same code. She dutifully prepared herself to make polite conversation.

He was already waiting in the restaurant when the Maître d' ushered her to his table. He stood politely, waiting until she sat before resuming his seat. After they had placed their orders, Angela cast around for polite conversation. "I'm intrigued, Mr. Aboud. There must be many casinos closer to your home country. Why travel all the way to Australia?"

The man shrugged in a gesture of ennui. "I have been to many of those establishments, and still do on occasion. Here, I am not so well-known, and I like that. The press are not reporting on my movements, nor is my father monitoring me so easily. It's my escape."

"And do you get to see much of the country? There's a lot more to see than the gaming tables."

"So far only the Sydney Opera House, Uluru and the Great Barrier Reef. Your country is so big, I don't always have time for the travel required. Perhaps if you were to show me, I could make that time available."

He turned beseeching eyes on her, and fearing he was about to grasp her hand, she quickly moved both of them to her lap. "I can certainly arrange for a tour guide. My family and work commitments mean that I am not free to travel, but thank you for the suggestion."

"A pity. If you were able to travel, I could show you my country. That would give me great pleasure."

Two offers to visit that part of the world! Perhaps one day she would actually get there. She smiled, and looked forward to the end of the evening.

Stephen knocked on her office door the following morning, and without waiting for an invite, dropped into the visitor chair.

"Thank you for looking after Nasir Aboud. I'm sure he'll be back, even just to see you again. He asked me if you ever have time off to go travelling."

"No, Stephen, absolutely not. Customer service and hostessing duties do not extend to playing tour guide, presumably with benefits. I expect you to make that absolutely clear."

"I had a feeling you might say that, and don't worry. I've already told him the answer's 'No'. I dropped in to give you the good news though. I've heard back from my mother. The executive committee of the Foundation have agreed to subsidise Melanie Cornell."

"That's fabulous news Stephen. What happens now?"

"The offer will be put in writing. As you would expect, there are conditions associated with reporting how the funds are spent. If they accept, I believe legal documents will be forwarded, covering payment processes and obligations. They should get the letter of offer in a couple of days."

"But that's fantastic. You must have presented a good case to the Foundation. And what of your promise? Are you still going to add to the offer?"

"You should know I never renege on a promise. Yes, I'll top up the offer. The Cornell women should be able to access the treatment they seek. Whether it has the desired effect is out of my hands."

"Of course, Stephen. I'm so pleased with your news." On impulse, she planted a kiss on his cheek before departing to patrol the floor. He had regained some of the ground he'd lost in her estimation and it was wonderful news for Wendy. And for David, it belatedly occurred to her.

For once, she was home at a reasonable hour, and Angela and Mattie sat down for a meal together. Louise had left for the day, and the two of them were enjoying some mother and son time. She felt guilty: she hadn't spent enough time with him recently. There was much to catch up on.

A furious knocking at the door interrupted the meal. Mattie froze, his wide eyes reflecting his fear. Strange; she wasn't expecting any visitors. Angela pushed back her chair, reaching out to pat Mattie on the hand as she did.

"It's okay, Mattie. I'm sure they haven't come back." There was no need to explain who she meant. "Best you go upstairs though."

"I'm staying here." The boy's expression changed to a fierce scowl. "I won't let anyone hurt you."

The knocking came again, if anything a little louder. There wasn't time to remonstrate with him.

"Stay out of sight," Angela hissed, and turned towards the door.

"Who is it?" she called.

Thank goodness Jimmy had arranged for a security peephole to be installed. The movement activated lights had come on, and although distorted, she could make out the figure of a woman on the doorstep.

"It's Wendy Cornell. Open up!"

With a sense of dread, Angela unhooked the security chain and opened the door. This was clearly not a friendly visit. The woman standing before her was rigid, her gaze deadly. Anger radiated from her every pore. She almost quivered with it.

"Wendy—this is a surprise. Won't you come in?"

192

"You bitch!" the visitor spat. "How dare you cosy up to me and pump me for advice and information when behind my back, you were scheming to bring my husband down?"

Angela stepped back a pace, astonished. The blood drain from her face as her mind raced through different scenarios. Nothing quite made sense. Did Wendy know about the coaching services? Was that what she meant?

"What are you talking about?" Angela reached for the door to steady herself.

"Mum, who's that lady? Why's she so angry?" She hadn't heard Mattie creep up behind her. His voice mirrored her concern.

"Mattie, go back and finish your tea. It's all right— Wendy's a friend."

"Friend! I don't think so. My husband has lost his job because of you, and now he tells me he might have to sell the house as well. You've got a lot of answering to do."

Things had clearly not gone well for David Cornell, but what on earth had he said? It was difficult to know how to respond without dropping him further in the mess he'd created.

"Now wait a minute. I'm not responsible for David losing his job."

"So you admit you know him? You said nothing about that to me."

"Wendy, why don't you come inside? We can talk more comfortably there." Angela opened the door wider, to invite her in.

"I don't need to come in." Wendy drew a deep breath. "I just wanted to tell you I hold you responsible for wrecking our lives. David told me he had a plan for sending Melanie to the States, and you and your friends crushed it. Do you realise what you've done, what you made him do? If you think you're going to succeed in the beauty industry, forget it. I'll make sure your name is mud." Her lips curled into a grimace. "Nobody will have anything to do with you after I've finished."

12 – A Misunderstanding

Angela watched as Wendy stormed off to her car. When she pulled out from the kerb, she barely missed the vehicle parked in front. Angela winced as she shut the door and retreated to the sanctity of the kitchen. That had not gone well. She'd lost an ally, David had lost his job, and possibly her dream was over before it had really begun. Would she be stuck at the casino forever?

"Has she gone, Mum? What did she want?" Mattie's pale face and big eyes reflected her own emotions.

"I don't really know Mattie. She has had some bad luck in her life and thinks in part that I'm responsible. It made her angry and she wanted to take it out on someone, and tonight it was my turn."

Angela made a cup of coffee while she pondered the situation. Whatever David Cornell had told his wife, it wasn't good. How dare he do that to her, after she'd done her best to salvage a situation that could have been much worse. After all, they'd kept the police out of it.

On impulse, she rang him. She didn't ring on Angelique's phone, in case he recognised the number and refused to pick up.

"David, it's Angela Benson."

"Who?"

"*Angelique*. I've just had a visit from your wife; a very hostile visit. What have you said to her?"

"I'm so sorry about that. I was in a bind and didn't know what to say. She kept asking questions."

"Surely you were prepared for that? Of course, she was going to ask you questions, you imbecile! Your problems are nothing to do with me."

She heard his sigh. "No, they're not. At least the company isn't taking legal action because they don't want the negative publicity, but it's the end of my career in the financial sector. I've promised to make restitution, and to do that I've got to sell the house."

"So how did my name come into the conversation?"

"I didn't mean to do it. Wendy knew I was having financial difficulties, but not the full extent, or why. I'd previously told her that I had a plan to deal with it, and then I had to tell her the scheme had failed."

"It was doomed to fail. Blind Freddy could have seen that. Did you tell Wendy about your role in all this? How you planned to use your connection with me to your advantage? How you planned to kidnap Stephen Lundy? No? I didn't think so."

"You're right, I know. I didn't want to give her all the details but I said the plan was thwarted by a woman and her group of friends. It never occurred to me Wendy could join the dots, so when she demanded to know who the woman was, I said you were a friend of Sasha and Renato Berkowitz, and that your name was Angelique." His sigh came over the phone. "She asked me what you looked like and somehow put two and two together."

If she'd been speaking to him in person, Angela would have shaken him. How could he have been so stupid? This was the man whose opinion she'd sought in the past and valued. "Just so you know, David, the Lundy foundation has agreed to provide a grant to your wife and daughter to travel to the States for Melanie's treatment, and I've persuaded Stephen Lundy to add to that. Wendy should get correspondence confirming that any day."

She paused, allowing the words to sink in, running her hand through her hair. "Now Wendy thinks I'm responsible for ruining your precious scheme, and in retaliation, she's determined to sabotage my new business. David, I am not responsible for getting you into this mess. You've done that all by yourself. You need to get Wendy off my back."

"Oh God, Angelique, I'm so sorry. I never meant for any of this to happen. I'm really grateful for what you've done. The quicker I can get Wendy out of the country, the less time she has to do any damage, but I'll talk to her tonight."

"You'd better. Make sure you tell her if it weren't for Angela Benson and her friends, you'd be in jail and the trip to America wouldn't be happening."

She disconnected the call without waiting for his response. To continue would only make her angrier and Wendy would probably be home soon. She had to think this through.

After dropping Mattie at school the following morning, she turned the car in the direction of Sasha and Renato's house.

Renato opened the door before she had the opportunity to knock, sweeping her into a warm embrace. "Angelique, this is a wonderful surprise this morning. Come in. We are having breakfast on the terrace. You will take some coffee? A croissant perhaps?"

"I'd love a coffee, particularly if you're making it."

She made her way through the house to the back terrace, where she found Sasha seated at breakfast and scrolling through the morning news on her iPad.

The older woman raised her face so Angela could kiss her cheek. "Lovely to see you, my dear. How are things with the new job?"

Angela described her days and some of the more noteworthy events. It filled in the time until Renato joined them with coffee, and in spite of Angela's protestations, a wicker basket containing heated croissants.

Angela wiped flakes of pastry from her chin. "As you've probably guessed, there is something I need to talk over with you. The casino role is not my preferred option, but it's a means to an end, and it will serve that function admirably."

"It will provide plenty of stories to dine out on," said Sasha, "but you have a problem?"

Angela told them about Wendy's visit and her subsequent discussion with David Cornell.

"I can't let her disrupt my plans. I've got to get started on it now. If I don't, it will never happen. I've decided to rent out the apartment. After all, I'm not using it much at the moment, only for doing some study and I can do that elsewhere—in my room at the Casino if I have to."

"That sounds sensible," said Renato. "You must make your investments work for you."

"I want to bring forward my business ideas. When I leave here, I'm going to the Salon to make them an offer. That's what I want to talk about. I have enough for a down payment, but I'll need to get a loan to complete the transaction and to be able to undertake the fit-out and start the marketing campaign."

This was where the hard part of the conversation came. "Bank lending policies have tightened a lot recently. If they ask for a guarantor, Renato, will you step in for me?"

Sasha and Renato sipped their coffee and focussed on their breakfast in silence. Angela didn't even see them look at each other but she could swear there was some sort of communication going on.

"Well now," said Renato, "This is something we can discuss. First you go and make your offer for the salon, and if it's accepted, then we will talk about it. Make sure you make the offer subject to finance."

With that, the topic was finished and Angela knew better than to pursue it further. Sasha and Renato acted according to their own rules. Glancing at her watch, she finished her coffee and stood. Time to visit the salon.

Angela was delighted to find a free car park close to the premises. It was a good omen. As she pushed open the door, she was met with tranquil music and a scent of indefinable floral notes.

"Morning, Angela. Lorna is taking care of bookings this morning, so we're free to chat. Come through."

She led the way past curtained cubicles to a small room at the rear. The shelves lining the walls were haphazardly stacked with a variety of products either used in treatments or sold to clients. Gracie shoved a pile of papers aside on the desk and moved more from a chair before inviting Angela to sit down.

"Excuse the mess. I've been catching up with bookwork and reviewing the accounts payable. It's a soul-destroying task. Can I offer you a cup of herbal tea?"

"Umm—a glass of water's fine, thank you." Angela surreptitiously took in her surroundings without wanting to stare. "You're looking well. How's the pregnancy?"

"Good, but I'm getting tired. I'm letting Lorna do more of the work so I can keep off my feet." She looked expectantly at Angela. "You said you wanted to discuss something with me?"

Damn. I should have thought this conversation through before rushing it. Angela took a sip of water before replying. "During a recent appointment, Gracie, you mentioned wanting to spend more time with your growing family. That comment stayed with me and I've been thinking it over. I'd like to make you an offer for the business, subject to examination of the books and a valuation."

There was a stunned silence. From her expression as she regarded her visitor, Gracie was clearly astonished. "You've taken me by surprise. I'm always being asked to provide sponsorship or vouchers for events focussed on women, and I thought that's what you wanted to talk about. I didn't know you were interested in this line of work!"

"I didn't know myself until recently. I've wanted to make a few changes to my lifestyle and this is one option that occurred to me. There were a few possibilities I considered, but I kept coming back to this idea. Another option is that I open a salon from scratch, rather than buying an existing business."

She wasn't really considering that, but dropped it into the conversation anyway. Gracie shook her head as though to discount that suggestion. "I would need to talk to my accountant. I've no idea how to put a value on the business. I don't own the building of course; I lease the premises."

Angela smiled politely but chose to remain silent. If she spoke now, she might interrupt Gracie's line of thought.

"I need to think about this a while. I've toyed with the idea of putting it on the market but hadn't decided. With the new baby and all, perhaps the timing's perfect. Lorna needs to be looked after though. She's been with me for ages." She broke off, her face a study of contemplation. "Can I call you about this? The price would have to be right before I gave it serious consideration."

"Of course. I didn't expect an immediate answer. I hadn't considered Lorna, but I would need skilled technicians working here, so there's no reason why she shouldn't stay on." Angela picked up her bag and stood. "You have my number, so call me when you want to discuss the details. What I will need to see are the financial statements for the last couple of years, and details of the lease you have on the premises. I'm happy to sign a confidentiality agreement if you require that."

Gracie walked to the front door with her. The two women shook hands on parting, with promises to 'talk soon'.

It had gone well. Angela was sure of that. She reviewed the conversation as she drove away. Gracie hadn't thrown a bucket of water on the suggestion, and judging by her comments, appeared to be thinking positively about a potential sale. Hopefully, she would be in touch soon.

It was lunchtime when she arrived at the Casino, but all was quiet.

"Any dramas Celia?"

The young woman barely looked up from her computer monitor. "Dead quiet today. Make the most of it. We've a party checking in later this afternoon, so that might require your support, but not necessarily."

"Fine. I'll do a quick tour of the floor, and then retire to my room to do some study. Can you order me a plate of sandwiches and some fruit? Call me if you need me."

The first thing she did after shutting the door behind her was to call Sasha.

"I'm feeling really positive. Gracie didn't throw me out—she took the suggestion seriously. When she calls me back, I'll be able to review the finer details and make a firm offer. The research I've already done will form the basis of that price, but I'll tailor it according to any further information."

"Well done, darling. Keep us posted."

It was hard to focus. Although she had an assignment to complete, she found herself working instead on a business plan for Maison Angelique. Her big fear was still that Wendy Cornell might have time to make good on her promise to blacken her name in the industry. Lucky she hadn't disclosed which business she wanted to buy.

By afternoon tea time, her head was swimming. The kitchen delivered a coffee and small sweet treat and she adjourned to the balcony for some fresh air and a break. It wasn't quite the view she was used to at her apartment, but was still a pleasant vista of the city.

It was a natural progression from thinking about the apartment to thinking about Luke. He was no longer Mr. Thursday. In getting to know him outside of their assignations, he'd assumed a different persona. Perhaps it was the fact that she now saw him with his clothes on. On reflection, that was a pity; the clothing hid a magnificent physique.

She nibbled around the edges of her biscuit, and then brushed the crumbs from around her mouth. It was an oddly sensual action and in her mind, it was Luke's finger gently brushing rather than her own. Then, his hand would move from her lips, past her chin and down to her neckline and décolletage. A gentle breeze sent wisps of hair on a dance around her face, creating their own tantalising, caressing sensation.

The thought of his return gave her a little frisson of delight. Would she experience that touch again? Perhaps things would progress on a different level on his return. A girl could dream.

She swept the tendrils aside and turned back to her room and her work. She was silly to waste the quiet time. It was unlikely to last.

The afternoon arrivals put paid to the time in her room. A call from Celia summoned her to the reception area.

"That group is in the process of booking in, Angela. Did you want to show them to their room?"

"Yes; I'll be with you shortly."

The group comprised an American couple and their two bodyguards. Angela knew from the briefing she'd received that they visited about four times a year.

"Mr. and Mrs. Adamson, welcome back to Casino Royale. I'm Angela Benson and if there is anything I can do to make your visit more comfortable, please let me know. The porter will show you to your rooms. Would you like room service to bring you some refreshments, or would you like to rest after your flight?"

"Thank you, Angela," Flora Adamson replied. "If you could send Perrier water and a dish of pink grapefruit to the room, that would be wonderful. I think I will rest for a while. My husband may have his own ideas."

The woman laid her hand on Angela's arm and leant closer. "Tell me, my dear—do you know a good salon you could recommend? I always like to get a facial after a long flight. Those aircraft cabins are so dehydrating."

If only I could recommend Maison Angelique!
"Certainly. Would you like me to make an appointment for you? When you're ready, I'll order a driver to take you there."

With arrangements made, and the guests taken care of, Angela completed a quick tour of the floor before returning to her office to check the calendar for details of other guests and any requirements they might have, either stated or anticipated.

Mr. Aboud was one of them. He had spent a day at another Casino interstate, but was booked in to Casino Royale again that evening. As he had mentioned over the dinner they'd shared, he felt that patronising different establishments gave him a greater percentage of winnings. Didn't the man ever have to work? She'd not asked him about that aspect of his life, not wanting to be intrusive.

Stephen poked his head around the door late afternoon. "I wanted to let you know I'll be flying out tomorrow. I have meetings both in Singapore and China, then I have to stop off in Europe followed by a week in New York. It will be hectic, but you've got my number. If there are any problems, give me a call."

"And the Foundation—have they written to Wendy Cornell?"

"I'm not involved with their operations, so I've no idea. I'll call my mother if that helps."

"Thank you, Stephen, I'd appreciate it. I can't explain now, but the sooner Wendy has that aspect of her life sorted, the better."

"Got it. I must run. I'm meeting the Adamsons in the Cocktail Lounge."

Angela rose and walked with him to the door. She was intending to do another tour of the facilities before ringing her mother with the time she expected to be home. "I hope your trip is successful. Don't work too hard."

Mr. Aboud was hovering by the reception desk, waiting for Celia to finish a phone call. He wheeled around when he saw them.

"Ah, Stephen; Miss Angelique… how fortuitous to see you."

Stephen shook the other man's hand in greeting. "Pleased to see you back, Nasir. I hope you've been well-looked after on this visit to Australia?"

"Indeed, I have. Miss Angelique is very attentive. I have been grateful for her helpfulness; in fact, I wanted to invite her to join me for dinner tonight."

Angela's heart sank. She didn't want to encourage the man. This could get tricky. She tried to catch Stephen's eye without being obvious about it. She was overdue spending a night with Mattie. At this rate, he would forget what she looked like.

"I'm sure she'd be delighted," Stephen said. "We have a new chef in the restaurant; you must tell me what you think."

He turned back to Angela. "Don't forget to call if you need anything." He leant forward and kissed her on the cheek and hurried off, followed by Angela's silent curses. She composed her face and turned to Mr. Aboud. "It's very kind of you to offer, Mr. Aboud, but tonight I should be home with my family."

"Oh but this will be my last night in your country. I fly out in the morning. I would be heartbroken if you were not able to dine with me."

Damn. At least he was leaving the country and her plans were advancing. With a bit of luck, the situation wouldn't arise again. "Let me make a phone call. I'll catch up with you in the gaming room shortly."

He disappeared in the direction of the tables, and Angela slipped back into her office to call her mother. Although she was sure it would not be a problem if she was late, she was loathe to take Louise for granted.

"Not a problem, dear. Mattie and I will be fine."

Pity. There was no reason to refuse.

She sought Mr Aboud out and agreed to meet him later in the dining room and after completing the disrupted circuit of the floor, returned to the sanctuary of her room to complete her assignment. She was less likely to be disturbed there than in the office.

Thank God for Business Class. It had been a long-haul flight, but Luke had managed to get some sleep. He still felt like yesterday's news. With his affairs wrapping up earlier than expected, there was no point in hanging around. He was keen to get home.

He'd called ahead to Maria to let her know his time of arrival, and Jimmy had turned up to the airport to pick him up. That was a nice surprise. Better than a taxi. Even more surprising was the cup of coffee Jimmy had waiting for him, and a copy of the day's paper.

"I thought you might like to catch up on what's been happening on the local scene while you've been away."

"Thanks Jimmy. What about the news that won't be in the papers? Anything to report?"

"Everything's gone quiet." He laughed derisively. "No more trouble from the 'Russian mafia', but I didn't expect there would be. Those blokes know better than to bother us again. I believe Mr Cornell is looking for a new job, and also that his wife and daughter are departing shortly for America. Any more than that, you'll have to ask Miss Angelique."

"I'll certainly do that." Luke kept his gaze straight ahead. "And how is she, now the drama has settled down?"

"I haven't seen much of her since she started the new role at the Casino. Best you ask her yourself."

"I might do that, after I've dumped my luggage and had a shower. I must smell like last week's washing."

"I wasn't going to mention it, but since you've brought it up…" Jimmy took his eyes off the road long enough to deliver a teasing grin.

The two men laughed companionably. In spite of his tiredness, Luke felt good. Engaging Jimmy was a great idea.

Maria greeted him as though he'd been away for a year instead of only weeks. Luke could smell good things happening in the kitchen, and knew they'd started as soon as she learned he was on his way. First step though was a

208

shower, and second step was to speak to Angela. He'd brought back a present as promised, and had plenty of time on his homeward flight to plan what he was going to say. The future was looking good; he could feel it in his bones.

When she entered the dining room, Nasir Aboud was already seated in a table by the window. City lights were reflected on the surface of the river, creating a magical backdrop. He stood to greet her, taking her hand and kissing it. In another situation, it could have been a romantic gesture, but now it made her feel vaguely uncomfortable. The maître d' pulled out her chair, and she slid into it with a polite smile for Nasir and a nod to the staff member.

Angela drew on all her past experience in making conversation, and helping her companion feel he was fascinating and wonderful company. In this situation it wasn't so difficult, as Nasir Aboud was not lacking in confidence.

"I am so pleased you were able to change your plans this evening. I am sure it will be a most pleasant evening for you."

"Indeed, Mr Aboud. I knew it would be."

"Nasir, please. We should not stand on such formality." He nodded to the waiter to top up their wine glasses. "I hope I can persuade you to visit my country some time; then you can meet my family and I can take you to see all the sights."

"I don't think that will be possible in the short term, but thank you for the offer—Nasir."

The meal wasn't as onerous as she feared. Nasir was an attentive companion, and entertained her with stories of his travels and experiences in Australia. The discussion was wrapped around the arrival of their dishes, each exquisitely prepared and a visual work of art.

It wasn't a late evening. The card she often pulled was that her baby sitter was on a time limit, and she couldn't be home late. There was no reason to hide Mattie's existence in this situation.

"I understand. Children are very important. You are lucky to have a son. Before you go, however, I have a small gift for you."

"Nasir, thank you for the thought, but I neither need or expect presents. If I do my job well, that is the only gratitude I require."

"Yes I am aware of that, and of course you are most professional in how you conduct yourself. It is only something trifling. It would give me great pleasure if you accepted this small token."

Reaching into the pocket of his jacket, he pulled out a small box and passed it over the table. Angela froze. Surely it wasn't a ring? There must be casino policy about not accepting gifts from guests.

"Please open it, Miss Angelique."

Reaching across the table, she slid the box towards her and opened it. Inside was a pendant, featuring what she assumed was a smallish diamond in a gold setting, and suspended on a gold chain. It was beautiful.

"Nasir, I can't accept this. It is beautiful and very thoughtful of you but employees cannot accept presents." She hoped that was the case.

"I will speak to Stephen myself. He cannot deny me this small pleasure. Please, try it on."

Faced with the inevitability of the situation, she tried to secure the necklace, fumbling with the catch."

"Allow me." He jumped up and moving behind her, took the chain from her grasp and adeptly fastened it as she held her hair to one side. He then stood back to admire the effect. "Beautiful; truly beautiful."

"Isn't she just!"

The voice was unmistakable. Looking around, Angela was flabbergast to see Luke standing a couple of metres away, with an expression that spoke derisive volumes.

"Luke! I didn't expect to see you here."

"That much was obvious." He turned and abruptly left, the plush pile of the carpet masking what was a most emphatic exit.

13 – New Business Option

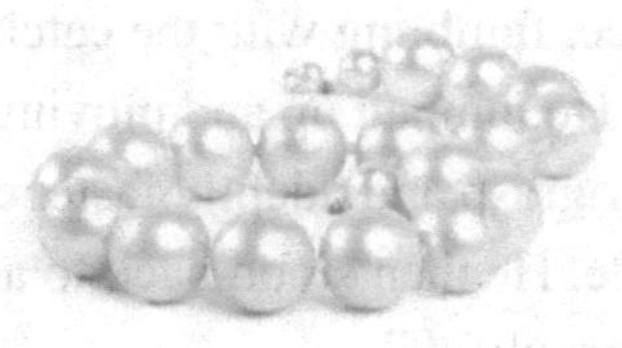

"Did Luke catch up with you?" Louise looked up and muted the television program as Angela came in the front door. "He rang here early evening. I told him you were working back at the Casino and he said he would drop in and surprise you."

"He definitely surprised me, and not in a good way."

"Oh dear; I should have called to let you know he was coming."

"Not your fault, Mum. It was an unfortunate set of circumstances"

She shed her coat and kicked off her shoes. She needed to be comfortable for this phone call. Retreating to her room, she dialled his number. Would he pick up?

"Angelique; how nice of you to call."

He wasn't addressing her as Angela. That in itself was telling. "You can call me Angela now. Why didn't you tell me you were coming?"

"I thought I'd surprise you—*Angela*. I brought back a gift for you and Matthew and decided to drop them into you at work. Instead, I found Angelique entertaining a client. Does Lundy get a cut now?"

"Luke, I've told you about my work. I'm employed by the Casino to look after the Presidential clients."

"It's a little more than that from what I saw. Gifts for services given, it seems. Is that the next step up from executive coaching, servicing the rich and famous?"

She suppressed a gasp. "Luke! That is unforgivable. Mr. Aboud is a respected guest at the Casino. I was having dinner with him, nothing more."

"If you say so."

"How can you say things like that? If you won't believe me, there's no more to be said. Goodbye Luke." She disconnected the call not waiting for his response.

If she could cry, there might have been some relief from the chokingly tight bands that bound her chest. Just breathing was an effort. It wasn't supposed to be like this. She sat for a long time, replaying recent events in her mind and thinking of the future, what she had hoped and what it would be.

Sleep didn't come easy that night, and when Angela awoke, it was with a headache. The new day also brought renewed resolution. She didn't need any man in her life. Not Stephen Lundy, not Nasir Aboud and particularly not Luke Johnson. Mattie was man enough.

Making up for working back the previous night, she decided it could be another late start at the casino. She made a list of things to do to keep focussed. If Gracie didn't come to the party, she would find new premises and start from scratch. A feeling of urgency drove her decision. There would be no existing good will, but she would deal with that.

Securing operating capital was an immediate priority. She had to cover the cost of branding, refurbishment, developing a social media presence, and the promotional campaign. Then there was the hi-tech equipment she'd learned about. That would take serious money. As soon as the bank was open, she rang and made an appointment with the lending manager for later that morning. That was one tick off the list.

The next call was to Sheldon Weybourne.

"Angela—I wasn't expecting to hear from you this morning." His voice was far from welcoming.

"You mean you were hoping not to." The brief pause confirmed her suspicions.

"I *was* surprised in what I heard," he agreed, "and disappointed as well."

"Sheldon, I know Wendy has worked for you for a long time, and you have a loyalty to her. I'm not able to disclose everything, but I can tell you Wendy is mistaken in her understanding of what or who was responsible for her husband's current predicament. Her fortunes will take a turn for the better, but again I can't talk about that either. Can you not shut me out just yet?"

"What Sasha told me about you didn't equate with what I heard from Wendy," he agreed. "I'll reserve judgement for now. What can I do for you?"

"I've done my research and Wendy—when she was speaking to me—was very helpful. I've worked out what products I want to stock. If I send you through a list, can you

214

cost them for me? I'm keen to move forward on this venture."

"Have you secured your premises?"

"Yes," she lied. "It's got the green light."

Part of her strategy was to start as she meant to continue, and that meant being positive and promoting the image of success from day one. That was important, not just to counteract any scuttlebutt from Wendy but as part of her PR campaign.

"Email it to me," Sheldon said, "and I'll get back to you. Best if you only deal with me for now."

That was another tick off the list, even if he had reservations. She gathered up her financial paperwork, and with a kiss goodbye to Louise, left for her appointment with the bank. It was a challenge quelling the nerves in her belly, but image and the appearance of confidence went a long way in these meetings. She focussed on both.

She was shown into the manager's office and invited to sit down. Welcoming posters with smiling, happy employees adorned the walls. The woman possibly never looked at those pictures. Her demeanour was solemn, and except for the obligatory handshake and greeting, her expression remained impassive as she flipped through the financial application.

"Tell me, Ms Benson—what experience do you have in running your own business?"

This could be tricky. "I've been providing executive coaching services for three years."

Her clients always paid in cash. She filed tax returns, but not all of the money was accounted for.

"Your banking history with us does not indicate a strong level of activity."

Yes, but… she wanted to say, but how could she explain? "I can provide guarantors if that's necessary, and I also have a reasonable share portfolio." She had purchased the apartment in her company name, and so couldn't claim that as *her* asset.

The woman put down her pen, and now looked her directly in the eye. "You've done your homework and it's an interesting proposition. It's still a risky venture however and in the current economic climate, the bank is not in the business of taking risks. Come back when you have more capital behind you."

It was not the news she'd expected. Humiliating tears pricked at the corners of her eyes as she climbed back into the car. The journey into work was made on automatic pilot as she reviewed the conversation and the implications. She couldn't just abandon the concept, but how to get around the lack of money? She was just pulling into her car park at the casino when her phone rang.

"Angela? It's Gracie. Are you free to talk?"

"Sure, I'm in the car, but I've just stopped. Go ahead."

"I've just come back from a medical appointment. My blood pressure is going through the roof and if I don't get it under control, I'll have to go into hospital until the baby's born. I don't want to do that, so it's made up my mind. I'm going to sell the business."

"Okay, that's a good reason." Angela's mouth was dry. She'd been hoping for this call but now that it had come, she was taken by surprise.

216

"I need to know if you're still interested, as my husband is insisting I list it today with a business agent if you don't want to go ahead."

"Yes … yes, of course I am. As soon as you can provide me with the paperwork I mentioned, we can agree on a price."

"I'll get onto that straight away. Can we meet tomorrow? I'll have the information ready then. It gives me the rest of the day to work on it."

They completed arrangements and disconnected the call. Angela's brain raced a million miles per hour as she sat and thought about the assurance she'd given. There was an obvious solution to the financial shortfall. She would have to sell her share portfolio. It was her least preferred option, given the time and effort she'd spent building it up, but what else could she do? Asking Sasha and Renato to be guarantors was one thing, but asking them for a loan could sully the relationship.

The die was cast. The business had to be a success, and then she could build up the portfolio again. No pressure. She climbed out of the car and strode towards the casino elevator with more confidence than she felt.

After firing up her laptop, Angela logged onto her trading account and listed all of her holdings for sale, then rang a real estate agent who she'd met through Sasha to make arrangements for the apartment to be let. She was committed. She had to negotiate a successful purchase now.

She massaged her temples and considered the enormity of what she was doing. The ring tone from her phone broke her reverie. She glanced at the screen. It was Luke. She had nothing to say to him. She tapped the reject key and let the call go through to voicemail. There was work to be done. She listened to the message later that afternoon.

"Angela, I need to talk to you."

Well, I don't need to talk to you. She deleted the message.

A strange car sat in the driveway when she arrived home that evening. At least it wasn't a black Volvo. She was still cautious on opening the front door.

"Cara Angela—so good to see you!" Maria grabbed her and kissed each cheek after she walked into the kitchen. "Your mother has been giving me all your news. Now you are a fancy casino lady."

"Not for much longer, Maria. I have plans! When I can tell you, you'll be the first to know— after my mother of course."

The coffee cups and remains of a plate of biscuits indicated the two women had been chatting for a while.

"Maria brought some of her biscotti," Louise said, "and guess what? Luke's engaged Jimmy as his security consultant, supervising operations both here and overseas."

That was wonderful and more than she'd suggested. "I'm really pleased for Jimmy. I've missed him since commencing work at the Casino. Missed his coffee too."

"No worries. I will cook dinner for you all," Maria said. "I'm sure Mr. Luke will be pleased to see everyone again. He will also be interested in your news."

"Perhaps, but my work schedule is demanding and unpredictable." It was easier to remain non-committal than to refuse, inviting questions about 'why not'.

218

Angela decided against working the following day. It was a flexible job after all. There was too much to do. She dropped in on Sasha and Renato and told them their guarantees would not be required.

"But what will you do? How can you proceed with the purchase if the bank won't support you?"

"You probably won't like this, Renato, but I've put my share portfolio on the market. When the business turns over a profit, I'll build it up again."

She expected a roasting on being stupid, but to her surprise he shook his head, but not in a bad way. "Angelique, you are a very determined woman. I am sure you will make a success of your little venture. I would have preferred you didn't sell, but now you will work very hard. You will have to. I will watch your progress with interest."

Sasha kissed her on both cheeks. "I wish you all the luck in the world. Make this a big success, Darling. It is a wonderful opportunity."

With their backing and encouragement, her steps were much lighter when she met with Gracie and her husband. The couple supported each other in the negotiations, but it helped that they were keen to reach agreement. Angela had also done her homework. Her opening offer wasn't accepted, but the final price they agreed on was reasonable to them all. It was still subject to closer examination of the documentation that Gracie provided.

In reality, Angela was not terribly fussed about it. She was determined to make a success of the business based on her own business plan, rather than past performance under the current ownership. They shook hands on the deal, with the promise of a champagne celebration after the baby was born.

"I'll still be calling you for advice, Gracie. It's such a change in direction for me. I'm both excited and terrified at what I'm doing."

"From what I've seen of your confidence in our negotiations, you'll be fine. You'll have Lorna to steer you in the right direction, but feel free to call me any time. Given the way my legs are swelling, I'll probably be in for a foot massage."

"Done deal! You'll get the deluxe treatment."

Gracie promised her solicitor would deliver a contract on the agreed terms by the end of the week. At the end of the month, the business would be hers. Viva Maison Angelique!

The apartment had to be cleared out next. There wasn't much to remove. She was letting it furnished and didn't have many personal belongings there anyway. She cleared out the fridge, the bathroom and the wardrobe. With the car loaded, she paused to take in the view from the balcony one last time. It was so beautiful. She would miss it—and the company she'd had. Providing her executive services had been a job, but there were certain side benefits. She had genuinely liked them all, even the recent Mr. Wednesday.

Her thoughts on Mr. Thursday were bitter sweet. The man had the ability to ignite passion in her more than any other. She so desperately missed his touch, his tongue... even his scent. Dammit, she missed the man, not just the sexual encounters. It was his mind and that innate strength that made you believe he would succeed in anything he did. The catch was, he only saw her as Angelique, provider of unique coaching services. She slid the balcony door shut, and left the apartment, locking those memories behind.

The next couple of weeks were chaotic. Angela still had to work at the Casino, both days and nights, according to demand. Until the business transferred to her name, there was nothing she could do to the premises, beyond planning. Anyway, she needed all the money her salary provided. Celia was her sounding board as she had to make some of the decisions.

" I'm happy with the colour scheme, but what do you think of these font choices for the branding? The designer has given me a couple of different options."

"I like them both. This one's more formal, but that one has a sophisticated edge. Try standing back and looking at them from a distance."

The good part was the delay meant she had time to plan the interior design, and how to make the layout work best. What she would really like, once the business could sustain it, was to lease the adjoining premises as well. Previously a video shop, it was now empty and would provide all the space she envisioned.

"Gracie, has there been any interest in the shop next door?" she asked on one of their catch-up meetings.

"Not as far as I know. You'll have to ask the owner. I haven't met him but the managing agent told me this complex has been sold. Don't worry—the purchaser still has to honour the terms of this lease. Your tenancy is secure."

"That's good to know. I'll follow up on that. Do you mind if some tradesmen come in to view the premises and take some measurements? I'm getting quotes for refurbishment and I'm hoping to hit the ground running after settlement."

"As long as it's after hours that will be fine. I don't think clients will be happy if blokes are traipsing around while they're having treatments."

Angela laughed. "I should think not. I'll coordinate and get them all here at the same time."

A couple of days later over dinner with Sasha and Renato, she ran through the outline of her strategic plan.

"Like it or not, I have to keep working at the Casino for now. I've sold the shares and the quotes are coming in for refurbishment. I'm closing the doors for two weeks to allow work to be done, and of course to give me time to plan a fabulous opening party."

"Darling, that sounds so exciting," Sasha said. "Book me in for a facial. I'll be your first customer."

"Sasha, you'll have a free pass forever. I'll schedule regular appointments with my best beauty therapist, nail technician, masseur—the works. I owe you so much."

"You'll never make a profit at that rate."

"Yes, I will! Everyone will want to know about the establishment Sasha Berkowitz patronizes and will want to be seen there too."

"I don't know if I have such a loyal following but I hope you're right. I will be telling everyone I know."

The end of the month seemed too far away, and yet incredibly close. Angela had a lengthy 'to do' list and crammed as much as she could into each day. She couldn't wait for the moment when the business would finally be hers.

She took time off from the Casino to attend the solicitor's office, signing the paperwork and handing over a bank cheque. After all the drama and angst, it was almost an anticlimax.

Celia was more excited than she was and on her return, the staff gathered in her office for a glass of bubbles. Stephen was back in the country and even he dropped by.

"Don't think you can leave me this quickly," he cautioned. "You've fitted in so well here. The place runs more smoothly with your magic touch."

She smiled sweetly, but held her tongue. As soon as she could afford it, she would be out of there. Her experience at the Casino would become history.

That evening, she drove to the salon before driving home. Just sliding her key into the lock gave her a thrill. Switching on all the lights, she prowled in every corner before going back outside and looking up at the façade of the building. She had ordered a repaint in the new colour scheme, and then new signage was going up as well. She held the designer's sketch, imagining what the real thing was going to look like. Perfect, just perfect.

As she turned to go back inside, she had the feeling of being watched. A shiver crept up her spine. Ever since the incident with Mr Wednesday, she had been more jumpy than she cared to admit.

Glancing around, she noticed a car on the other side of the road. She couldn't see the driver as the windows were dark. That was ominous in itself but she couldn't shake off the feeling of being watched. Where was Jimmy when she needed him?

She strained to identify the car's make. She was just reaching for her phone to take a quick photo when the car pulled out from the kerb and disappeared into the dusk. By the time she got back inside, she could only remember the first three letters of the number plate. It was probably nothing. She was just being silly.

Not so silly she didn't think to call Louise. "I'm just on my way, Mum. I dropped past the salon after I left the Casino. I should be there in about twenty minutes. Any takers for a celebratory meal at Mario's?"

"I could ask that young man of yours, but I doubt he'll say no. See you soon sweetheart. We'll be ready and waiting."

The street outside was empty. No strange cars. She checked both ways, keys in one hand and phone in the other, before locking the door again and climbing in her car. Jimmy would be proud of her.

14 – The Launch of Maison Angelique

The first guests were arriving. Kitted out in a new tuxedo, Mattie took his meet and greet role seriously. He was only staying for a short time before Louise was taking him home, but in the early part of the evening, he greeted guests as they arrived.

Angela checked everything for the nth time. It was going to be a bit crowded, but they would have to cope. She had hired the adjoining premises for the evening, draping the walls with panels of material and banners gauzy in her theme colours of ivory and pink. Guests could be taken next door to the salon for a tour of inspection.

Sasha advised her on catering, and reviewed the guest list. Angela invited her new colleagues from the Casino, and also Jimmy, Maria, Stephen Lundy and his mother, and of course Sheldon Weybourne. Wendy was in the States. David Cornell didn't rate a mention. Sasha had added media representatives, fashion influencers, and some of the A-listers who often attended her soirees.

Angela had even invited the managing agent for the strip of shops, plus, through him, the building owner. She'd learnt her lesson well from Sasha on building and maintaining business relationships.

The one person she didn't invite was Luke Johnson.

Louise was puzzled by this and tried to talk her daughter around. "Don't you think, Angela, after all he did for us it would be a polite thing to do? Jimmy and Maria are coming—you can't leave Luke out of it."

"I can, Mum, and I will. Luke's behaviour since returning from his trip has been reprehensible. I don't want him at the opening."

Lorna and Julia, her new off-sider, were on duty for the evening. Julia had been with them for a week already, and specialised in laser therapies. Dressed in the uniforms she'd designed, they handed out goodie bags. They contained skincare samples, and vouchers for skin condition assessments and information about joining the *Maison Angelique Club*. It offered additional benefits to members, including eligibility to attend an annual health care and beauty retreat.

"Angelique—you did your research well." Sheldon Weybourne kissed her cheek. "I don't know the full story, but I heard you were instrumental in helping Wendy and her daughter to travel to the States. Thank you for that."

"My pleasure. She was so helpful; I really appreciate it."

226

"So does Wendy. She's heard about this event and wishes you well."

I wonder what Wendy told Sheldon? David must have told her the truth, or at least some version of it. She moved on before getting too embroiled in the conversation. There was an endless chain of meet-and-greets and cheeks to kiss, and the buzz in the air didn't come anywhere near the buzz she was feeling.

The photographer she'd hired moved through the crowd, capturing smiling groups and people of note. Angela was posing together with the editor of a social media magazine and a morning television presenter, when she saw him. He was watching her, and when they made eye contact, he inclined his head in a small nod of acknowledgement. In that instant, the world froze. The noise and chatter faded. She and the man on the other side of the room were in their own bubble.

"Smile, sweetie," the photographer cooed, and the volume around her was turned up again. The smile for the benefit of the photo felt more of a grimace.

It was some minutes before she could weave her way through the crowd of well-wishers to Luke's side, reaching him just as he swiped a glass of champagne from the wine waiter.

"You look wonderful," he said, raising his glass in salute.

"I didn't invite you." Her voice was flat. She looked past his shoulder rather than at him—anywhere rather than into those eyes.

"Yes, you did. I'm the owner of the complex. I understand you're interested in leasing these premises as well. You'll have to talk to me about it."

What the…? How could she not know this?

"I can't do that now," she replied stiffly. "I have guests to look after."

"Wait a moment." He reached out and touched her arm. "I haven't given you the gift I brought back from overseas."

He held out the small box. She hesitated. She didn't want to take anything from him.

"I said I would bring something back," he persisted. "Open it."

The box was decorated with colourful decals, typical of middle-eastern colours and patterns. Opening it, she found an intricate bracelet of gold floral filigree, in a distinctly regional design. It was beautiful. Reaching out a finger, she traced part of the delicate metalwork.

"It's stunning."

"Allow me," he said, taking the bracelet from her hands and directing her to hold out her arm.

With more expertise than she expected, he opened the catch and secured the bracelet around her wrist. His fingers brushed her skin as he did, with the sensation searing her. He held her hand a moment longer than was necessary. The memories of his touch came flooding back, overwhelming her with longing and the yearning she had fought to repress. This was not the time to explore those feelings.

"Thank you. I didn't expect anything." The moment was broken when the photographer bustled up with his camera.

"Can I take your photo? A little closer, please. Smile!"

228

Luke obligingly moved closer and with his arm around her waist, drew her against him while the shutter clicked around them. The heat from his body matched her own. A familiar aftershave scent tantalised her senses.

"I must look after my guests," she muttered, not daring to look at him. She swept away, conscious of his eyes on her and aware of the tell-tale flush of emotion.

The rest of the evening was conducted with reference to Luke's location, as though an invisible cord linked them. She was aware of where he was at all times and to whom he spoke. Although he spent his time circulating and chatting to people he knew, her intuition told her he was just as aware of her as she was of him.

"Darling, it has been a wonderful evening." Sasha embraced her as she and Renato were preparing to leave. "It's only a start, but the interest is strong. You had some major influencers here tonight."

Angela felt giddy with it all. "It's been a fabulous response, but there was free champagne. That interest still has to translate into bookings.'

"But it has." Lorna overheard their conversation. "When I took people next door to view the premises and explain the services, a few made forward bookings." She grinned. "I told them available appointments were disappearing fast, and if they didn't book then and there, they might be waiting a while."

Sasha nodded approvingly. "You'll soon earn your keep. Provided you deliver a superior service, you'll do well."

Angela rolled her eyes at the complicity of the pair of them. Their initiative was pleasing though. Guests gradually drifted off as the evening progressed. Finally, there was only Angela, Julia, and Lorna left—and Luke.

"Julia, Lorna—you don't need to hang around. We've cleaned up enough tonight. The rest can wait until the morning. Thank you both for your help."

The women left, leaving then only the two of them.

Luke leant against the wall, arms folded. "So now it's just us. Congratulations by the way. The venture does you credit."

"Thank you. No coaching services provided either, just to be clear."

He had the grace to look embarrassed. "I owe you an apology. I was totally out of line before. I plead jet lag and an overactive imagination. I was taken by surprise at the scene I interrupted."

"There was nothing in it."

"I know that now. I had a few words with Lundy tonight. He set me straight on your role, even if I hadn't figured out the situation for myself after a good night's sleep."

"It shouldn't have needed Stephen to speak up on my behalf."

"You're right. He only confirmed what I already knew. Can I make it up to you?"

There were ways she wanted him to, but wasn't that inviting trouble and heartache? "It's getting late. We should just finish up here and go home."

"I've got a better idea. Why don't we go somewhere to celebrate a successful launch?"

Her heart and her head raged an internal battle while he watched her with an intensity that was disconcerting. She

230

spoke before she could stop herself. Why not, but not the Casino!" She'd had enough of that environment for a while.

"Absolutely not the Casino. There's a new cocktail bar at the top of Southern Cross Tower. Why don't we take in the lights over a cocktail or two?"

"Do you mean like a date?"

"I guess I do. Is that allowed in the Rules?"

For the first time that evening, she looked him fully in the eyes. Yes, of course it is, her heart was screaming. She made him wait a beat, lips pursed as though considering the matter. "Circumstances can require that rules are reviewed. I think this is one of those occasions."

"My car's outside. Shall we go?"

As they neared the vehicle, her eyes widened and Angela wheeled around in surprise. "It was you! You were watching me!"

He opened the passenger door for her to get in. "Guilty as charged. Maria kept me updated on what you were doing, thanks to the gossip network. I wanted to see for myself."

"I think you've got a bit of explaining to do."

"Perhaps—over a drink."

~

Luke took her elbow as they stepped out of the elevator and guided her towards the picture windows. It gave him a legitimate excuse to touch her. He'd missed that contact too much. Angela gasped with delight. The lights of the city stretched below, with the twinkles stretching to the horizon and reflected in the glass of city buildings.

They secured a quiet table near the window, where it was possible to talk, and gave their orders to the waiter.

"So perhaps you can start by explaining how it is that you're now my landlord," Angela said. "I thought it was an entity called LJ Holdings."

"That's my investment company. I keep the different arms of my business quite separate."

She appeared to be pondering this fact. "So, when did you buy the complex? Why did you?"

Luke had wondered what her reaction might be to discovering he was her landlord. "By coincidence, I was chatting to a person called Sheldon Weybourne at an event hosted by Sasha Berkowitz. He mentioned this strip of shops as being a good investment opportunity, and I put in an offer before I went away. The transaction was settled in my absence."

The waiter arrived with their drinks, and their conversation paused until he withdrew.

"When I discovered who had become my new tenant, I took it as an omen of our continued association." Luke raised his glass in salute. "Here's to your new venture and a long partnership."

The potent liquid ignited a slow fire that spread throughout his body, with a pleasant and soporific effect. As he relaxed, it occurred to Luke it was a long time since he'd taken any time out for himself. He needed to make some changes.

Angela seemed more relaxed as well. "I don't usually consider a landlord-tenant relationship to be a partnership," she mused.

"As there are two parties to the agreement, by definition it has to be. Still, there are other types of partnership. Perhaps we could consider those."

"If you're thinking of becoming a beautician, you'll have to undertake training."

He snorted. "That wasn't on my mind, although I could provide a good massage service. I see from the brochures you'll be providing a therapist." The thought of massaging that body of hers was appealing.

Her eyebrows rose a level. "I'm trying to decide if that would encourage our clientele, or scare them off."

"I was talking about us, actually," Luke said, maintaining eye contact. "Us, and the future."

"Do we have a future?"

"If my opinion counts, we do, but it all depends on your perspective. I don't want to make assumptions about your feelings."

Angela swirled the liquid in her glass, watching the circular movement as though it might disclose the answers to her unasked questions. A myriad of emotions were reflected on her face, but he wasn't sure what she was thinking.

Luke searched for the right words. He leant closer. "Our meeting wasn't conventional, but I've always felt it went beyond Thursday afternoons. Was I fooling myself? Was I wrong in assuming your feelings for me were growing as mine were for you?"

She licked her lips with an appearance of nervousness. "No, you weren't wrong." Her voice was no more than a whisper. "Maintaining that level of relationship with you was one of the hardest things I've ever done."

She touched the bracelet, fingering the intricate patterns. She lifted her eyes to his. "Who do you see in your future, Luke? Angela or Angelique?"

He gave a snort of suppressed mirth. "Can't I have both? The woman I've come to know and love is not defined by name. She's multi-faceted, and that's what makes her so appealing."

Angela looked unsure of what she was hearing. "You know I come as a package. It's a case of love me, love my son."

"I wouldn't expect anything less." *More importantly, are you going to tell me what you feel for me?* "Do you know how hard it's been not seeing you for all these weeks? And then you wouldn't take my phone call!"

"With good reason," she protested.

"You're not going to let me forget that, are you? Is there some way I can make up for that?"

"Perhaps." She smiled wickedly. "I think you shouldn't drive after drinking that concoction. Did you know they have rooms here too? Why don't we check if there's a vacancy? I feel like celebrating in more ways than one."

The trail of clothes led from the door of the room to the bed. This was no slow, sensuous seduction. Theirs was a demanding and greedy love-making that demanded immediate satisfaction.

Pushing Luke back onto the bed, Angela straddled his body, positioning herself to maximise her pleasure as she

234

rode him. Her hair, pulled from the barrette, tumbled over her breasts in a cascading stream. Luke reached up to cup one breast as she reached the pinnacle, the other hand pulling her closer so he could kiss those lips, now parted in ecstasy. Only then did he seek his own pleasure, flipping her over and driving into that pulsating centre until his cry of ecstasy matched hers.

"My God," he groaned when finally able to speak, "it was worth the wait. Just so you know, I don't want to leave it so long again."

He slowly propped himself back on his elbows and rolled over onto his back, pulling her close.

"I take it from that comment you're planning on an ongoing relationship?" she teased.

He clamped a possessive hand on her thigh. "I want you. I want you in my life and by my side. I want you today and tomorrow and the day after that. Does that answer your question?"

She sighed and melted closer against him. She craved the security of the contact, skin against skin. "It answers every question for now. You'll have problems ever getting rid of me." She yawned. "Do you mind if we talk about our futures in the morning?"

Sleep was a welcome intervention. The next morning, he made good on his promise to provide a superior massage service, starting with her back and working down her body and to the outer extremities.

Angela moaned softly as he found the knotted muscles and worked his way through them. *If there is a definition of bliss, I've found it*. Those hands were working the most incredible magic. It was an effort to stay awake.

"You've passed the test," she murmured.

"Test? What test?"

"The partnership. If you can massage like that, you're in. You're on the payroll already."

15 – A Cruise with a Difference

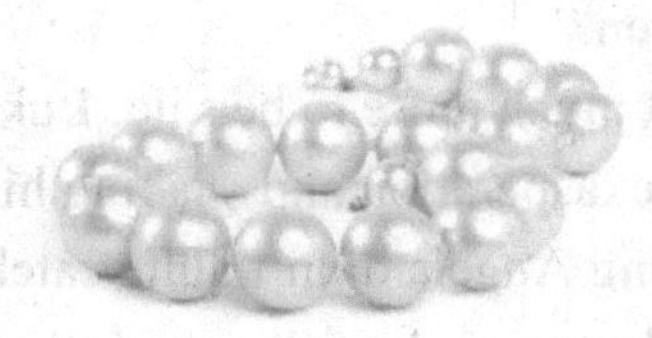

"The premises are mine. I can do what I want with them."
Luke's voice rose a level, his open-handed gesture
illustrating his point. A slight echo bounced off the walls,
thanks to the empty room. "If you want to expand the salon
into this shop, it's yours."

"I'm not taking the premises for free, Luke. I'll contact
the agent in the morning and ask him to prepare a lease under
normal commercial terms. Lorna will be so pleased. It's
partly due to her work that the salon has been such a
success."

"To hell with Lorna; it's you I'm thinking of." He took a
couple of paces towards the door and then swung back, his
hands on his hips. "If you won't let me lend you some
capital, at least I can do this."

Angela's folded arms and stony glare should have
warned him to back off. They'd already had this

conversation. It was time to move on. "We'll do this properly Luke, or not at all. I've never lived in any man's pocket and don't intend to start now."

"I like the idea of you living in my pants rather my pocket. What if taking help from me means you can quit working at the Casino?"

"Not even then."

There wasn't much more to be said. Luke glared at her, giving a snort of exasperation and shaking his head. He muttered something Angela didn't quite catch. They locked the door behind them and she followed Luke out to the car in silence.

"Your place?" he asked.

"Yes. Mum needs to get home. She's been looking after Mattie since she picked him up from school."

"You know, it doesn't have to be like this. You've seen for yourself; there's plenty of room at my house. If you and Mattie were living there, Maria would always be able to care for him after school. That would free up your mother."

Angela turned to look at him, a sudden lump in her throat. What was he suggesting? Only a live-in relationship of convenience? She squeezed her lips tightly together, repressing the eye-prickling surge of emotion, chastising herself at the same time. They'd been getting along so well, and secretly she'd hoped something permanent was developing between them, but not what he was suggesting. *I'm tired, that's all. I'm not in the mood to handle this.*

"Mattie needs stability in his life. He's a resilient kid, but recent events would have been disturbing for anyone. I'm not prepared to uproot him just yet."

238

Mattie was a convenient excuse. Angela knew he would love to live at Luke's house. Maria would spoil him rotten. He would imagine pancakes for breakfast every day of the week, and an endless supply of Lego. And then there was Luke. The small boy yearned for a man in his life, and eagerly anticipated Luke's visits, and the occasions when the three of them did something together.

She was the one who found the suggestion unsettling. *I can't let Mattie get too invested in this relationship. Isn't it bad enough that I love Luke, without Mattie developing stronger feelings as well? If I knew my feelings were reciprocated on a permanent level, that would be another matter, but...* She cut off those thoughts. No point in upsetting herself.

Luke looked at her quizzically when he pulled up outside the townhouse but didn't ask any questions. He probably sensed her mood.

She placed her hand on the door handle, ready to climb out, leaning across to give Luke a light kiss before she did. It seemed like forever since they'd exchanged more than that. Angelique had seen more of Mr Thursday than she had of Luke Johnson, in the three months since opening Maison Angelique.

She struggled to keep the sadness out of her voice. "Thanks for coming with me this evening. It helped to have someone to listen to my ideas."

"Any time," he replied dryly. "I'm not sure I had much to say though. I just listened and nodded on command."

"Glad you understand how it works." She flashed him a quick smile before opening the door. "I'll see you tomorrow evening. Don't forget we're going to the fund raiser."

"Wait a moment." Before she could lift a foot out of the car, Luke switched off the engine and reached for her. This time, his kiss was anything but light. As his tongue probed, meeting and dancing with hers, he slid a hand around her back and the other over her breast. Angela felt her nipple harden under the lace of her bra, causing her breath to catch. It made her feel very overdressed.

She strained closer, cursing the configuration of the car's bucket seats and separating console. She slid her hand inside his shirt, needing desperately to feel his skin. His heart was dancing a rhythmic beat that mirrored her own. Luke made a low growling noise, deep in his throat. *Easy tiger—I know how you feel.*

Whatever the confusing nature of their relationship, her body always responded positively to his touch. It was with supreme effort that she placed both hands on his chest, pushing a separating distance between them. She almost expected to hear a sucking sound as their lips parted.

"Whoa! Hold that thought until tomorrow night. If I don't go inside now, Mum will be out here rapping in the window like she did when I was a teenager."

Luke rolled his eyes, his chest still heaving. "Has anyone ever told you you're a cock tease?"

"Not for a while, but I can work on it."

She gave him a hooded look, and with a sultry smile, climbed out of the car, deliberately sashaying as she sauntered the path to her front door. She glanced back over

240

her shoulder and saw he was still watching her. With a wave of acknowledgement, he drove off. His tail-lights reached the corner before she turned the key and let herself in.

The morning brought with it the usual rushed activity. Angela had a meeting at the salon with Sheldon Weybourne. With Wendy being overseas, Sheldon was doing some of the salon visits. As if his internal antennae sensed his mother had to be out of the door by a certain time, Mattie dragged his feet. Lately he'd developed an attitude. What had happened to her sweet little boy?

"C'mon Mattie, finish your breakfast."

"Don't like it."

"But you ate it yesterday."

"I want pancakes."

"Mattie, you cannot have pancakes on a school day. I don't have time for this. Eat it, now!"

By the time she bundled him into the car and dropped him off at school, her nerves were frazzled. *How could I have thought opening the salon was going to be child friendly? What I need is a friendly child.*

She had little time to ponder the matter as Sheldon was already waiting in the reception area when she arrived. She took a deep breath outside on the footpath and paused a moment to put on her professional, in-control face before pushing open the door. She still felt an exhilarated thrill each time she stepped over the threshold. A soft blended scent of

Lavender, Sweet Marjoram and Chamomile drifted through the room, as an introduction to the relaxing bliss that waited.

"Sheldon, it's wonderful to see you again." She proffered her cheek for a kiss. "Has Lorna offered you a cup of tea or perhaps a soda spritz? I highly recommend the strawberry mint. Come on through to the office."

She ushered him over the plush carpet to the back room past the cubicles which were discreetly curtained off while clients received their treatments. Other clients, seated in recliner chairs, browsed magazines while waiting for their appointment. There was a quiet buzz about the salon, quite aside from the soothing background music. The room at the rear had been refurbished since she first saw it under a mountain of papers and product samples. It was now a place of well-ordered administration. A refreshing paint scheme in layers of cream and ivory and accents of pink created a professional ambience, and shelving lined the walls, with products used in treatments neatly arrayed.

"I've had enough tea for the morning, thank you. This is my first call for the day, so I've not long had breakfast." He took the seat she offered. "Business seems to be booming."

"It's better than I hoped," Angela agreed. "This is just the start. Now that I am taking over the premises next door, I can start on the big renovations. I'm planning deluxe treatment rooms with ensuite bathrooms, and even a spa room. The marble tiles for the wet areas should arrive any day."

"You've got grand ideas, but I like the exclusivity angle. It will reach a particular clientele." He glanced at the product shelves. "I'm expecting you'll need to re-stock. What can I help you with?"

"I'll call Lorna in. She'll have more idea, and she'll have to handle this in future anyway. Before I do, have you heard from Wendy?"

"I have, actually. She and her daughter are still finding their feet, and Melanie has commenced treatment. It'll be a while before there are any results, *if* the treatment works, but at least she's part of the trial. Wendy's grateful for the opportunity. She knows Luke Johnson has provided the accommodation and intends to thank him in person later."

She'll thank everyone except me; Angela Benson — the woman who made it all happen for her. "That's such good news. I hope it works out for them both. Still, it leaves you a bit short-staffed, doesn't it? How are you coping without her?"

Sheldon put his head on one side, regarding Angela speculatively. "That's something I wanted to talk to you about."

"Me? I'm still really busy at the casino. It's a short-term option, but soon I hope to be fully occupied with building up the business. I can't take on anything else."

Sheldon threw back his head and laughed, a rich baritone that erupted in a sharp burst. "Not you, Angela. Not that I wouldn't love to have you on board", he added hastily. "I was thinking of your mother."

"My mother doesn't work." Angela's tone betrayed her puzzlement.

"Not now, but I chatted to her at your opening celebration. She told me she'd like to get back into the workforce in a part-time capacity once your son doesn't need her anymore."

Angela blinked, processing what she'd just heard. It had never occurred to her that her mother might want to work again. Louise had quit her last job to help out when Mattie's father disappeared, and had seemed happy to do so at the time. *Why hadn't I thought to have this discussion with Mum?*

"It would be a steep learning curve," she said slowly, "but my mother would actually be rather good at it. I'll give her your contact details and ask her to get in touch with you. You can both take it up from there."

When Lorna joined them, she didn't need to be told what to do. She already had a list made out of what needed re-stocking and suggestions for what they might also order. Angela deferred to her experience, choosing instead to keep a tally on what it was all going to cost. She had to keep a tight control of expenses if she was going to have any hope of quitting the casino.

After Sheldon left, she and Lorna had a chat about the next month's marketing campaign. Angela had picked the brains of the marketing team at the casino, and had an overall strategy, but they still needed to put immediate plans in operation. She'd engaged a social media manager, wisely realising that she couldn't do everything—not yet anyway.

"I didn't want to discuss it while Sheldon was here, as I don't want our plans broadcast in advance, but I've arranged a permanent lease over the premises next door. I'll call the builder later today so we can start on refurbishment plans. It will mean creating a doorway between this shop and next

244

door, but I'll get that done over a weekend. I'd like to have it operational in time for Mother's Day."

"That's fabulous news." Lorna plonked herself in the chair Sheldon had just vacated. "You realise we're going to need more staff, don't you? Bookings for treatments are increasing, and if we're going to offer a wider range of modalities, we'll also need specialists in those areas." She tapped on the desk to emphasize her words. "We can give Julia more hours, but even with our existing range of services, we need more skilled technicians."

Angela sat back in her chair, lips pursed. Lorna was right, but more staff meant increased management responsibility. How would she cope with that? She couldn't stay at the casino much longer.

Business over the past three months had been brisk, better than she'd hoped. It meant she had trading figures to plug into her future projections. For not the first time, she gave thanks for her bookkeeping course. It had presented a range of options, meeting Sasha Berkowitz being one of them. Now she was in a better position to monitor her business affairs.

There was no time to dwell on it now though. She was due at the casino.

"You're right, Lorna. Leave it with me and I'll review the financials and see what's possible. We'll discuss the options after that."

She snatched a quiet moment at the Casino to look over her reports. Her analysis confirmed what she already knew. Following the launch, Maison Angelique was off to a flying start. It made her more confident about committing herself to the additional premises. Maybe she could think about building up her share portfolio again. One day perhaps, but for now she needed to maximise her operating capital.

The additional room would have to pay for itself from day one. Her gut twisted into a knot just thinking about it. She read back over her marketing plan to reassure herself. She couldn't afford to panic. The strategy was there—she just had to stick to the plan. She resolved to speak to the casino marketing team again to see if it needed tweaking.

That just left herself to consider. Could she give Stephen notice for the Casino role? She had come to rely on that support, even as she chafed at it. She just needed a little time in which to feel comfortable with the decision to leave.

The fund raiser was to support the swimming team at the Australian Institute of Sport. Mr Monday had forwarded her an invitation, which included a plus one. She'd hesitated to accept it, but rationalised she couldn't hide from her clients forever. She'd run into him at a fashion parade displaying swimming costumes from a local fashion house and using models who otherwise were swimmers training with the Institute.

The greeting had been enthusiastic, a little more perhaps than what the occasion called for but from him, anything less would have been surprising.

"Angelique!" He kissed her on the cheek. "Great to see you. I've missed you." He kept hold of her hands. "Is there any chance the Monday booking might become available again?"

This question was delivered with a cheeky grin, and much too loud for her liking. Angela looked around to see who was in listening distance. Lots of people, but hopefully they would have no idea what he was talking about. She took a step closer to him, half expecting to smell chlorine from the pool.

"Glen," she said sotto voce, "would you mind keeping your voice down? As I explained before, I am no longer providing those services."

"I thought as much," he replied, still with the same grin and still at the same volume. "You can't blame a man for asking."

Instinct told Angela he was about to do something incorrigible, like reaching out and squeezing her butt. She took a step back to ensure that didn't happen.

Before she could make her escape, one of the models came along and slipped her arm through his. With a smile and a wink, Angela took advantage of the distraction to move on. When she looked back a few moments later, his eyes were still on her. He gave a resigned smile, accompanied by a quick wink, and turned his attention back to the young woman at his side. Angela knew he would never ask again. She definitely hoped he wouldn't say anything in front of Luke.

Luke was her plus one at the evening's event. She was already hovering by the door of her townhouse when he drew up out the front in the Audi.

"Hi there, beautiful. You had better fill me in on the evening, and who might be there. How did you score an invite?" Luke pulled smoothly away from the kerb, and joined the flow of traffic. "I didn't realise you had such an interest in sport."

"You'd be surprised how extensive my interests are. I'm not only focussed on skincare regimes, you know." She glanced at him to judge how serious his question was, but had the impression it only passing conversation. "My network has broadened considerably since I started working at the casino. I meet people from all over the state and from every industry. The sporting fraternity is no exception."

It was the truth after all. There was no need to mention Glen never stepped foot in the casino and she would not disclose he had been a client. She explained about the Institute and its goals. She'd picked up quite a bit during her Monday conversations.

"Young people attend the Institute from all over the country. They're keen and talented, but don't always have much money. The fund raiser helps finance their travels when they need to compete away from home. It's a worthy cause."

"No arguments from me. I only hope the speeches don't go on too long."

You're not the lone ranger there. I'm happy to schmooze for a while, but don't want to hang around when I have other important things to think about.

When they arrived, Luke got out and tossed the keys to the valet. He opened her car door and offered his arm. "You're looking stunning tonight. I've always admired that

248

dress on you." He nuzzled her neck and sniffed appreciatively. "You smell gorgeous too."

"I hadn't expected you to remember the dress. I've only worn it once before." It was the blue sheath she'd worn the evening of Sasha's soiree.

"I remember everything you've worn; including when you haven't worn it at all." His voice was teasing, and pitched at a level for her ears only.

She rolled her eyes at him, but the twitch to the corner of her mouth was a stronger indication of her reaction. "You've an overactive imagination. Just behave yourself." She slowly and deliberately allowed her gaze to sweep over him. "Just remember two can play at that game. Come to think of it, you're looking rather debonair yourself. It could give a woman certain ideas."

"Promises, promises. Hold those thoughts." He placed a quick kiss on her cheek before escorting her towards the door and reception area. They joined the throng of people inside the venue, and ran into quite a few people they knew.

Glen was there of course. He spied Angela and broke away from the group he was with and made his way towards them. His eyes flicked over Luke before looking back to her. Angela caught her breath but Glen's smile was gracious and for once he was impeccably behaved.

"Angela, so pleased you could come." He kissed her lightly on the cheek before turning to Luke and holding out his hand. "Hi. I'm Glen Braxton."

"The swimmer?" Luke inclined his head in acknowledgement. "I'm Luke Johnson. Pleased to meet you. I hope your fund-raiser is a great success."

"I'm sure it will be, but any contributions will be gratefully received." Glen moved on to the next arrivals and they worked the room, chatting to other guests. There was entertainment provided with some big name singers who had donated their time. A well-known television presenter was the emcee for the event. It was generally a pleasant evening, with the glitterati and well-heeled who had paid handsomely to attend.

A silent auction ran through the evening. Sponsors had donated a range of prizes, and guests were invited to make their bids on selected items by writing their name on a form and the amount they were prepared to pay. Others who wanted to bid would have to nominate a higher amount if they wanted to secure the item. There was jewellery, a bottle of vintage Penfolds Grange, and some artworks. The Lundy Foundation had even donated a cruise on the Lundy family yacht, with a full complement of crew and chef on call. Guests were clustered around the bidding forms. Angela surmised the evening would be lucrative for the Institute.

There was nothing that particularly interested her. The cruise would be fantastic of course but her current goal was on economising, not opening her purse. Besides, the sooner her social obligation in attending the function was finished, the sooner she and Luke could politely depart. It was already arranged that she would stay with Luke that evening as her mother was looking after Mattie.

Some of the guests were also clients of Maison Angelique, and Angela made sure she spoke to those she knew, and sought their impressions of the salon.

"I was given a voucher for my birthday. It was the best present ever," one woman enthused. "I've made another booking for next week. I hope you start providing the massage service soon. I like the idea of a one-stop shop."

"I'm working on it. I'll ask Lorna to mark your file with a discount for your first massage."

That's another happy customer. I hope she tells all her friends.

As Angela smiled and schmoozed her way through the crowd, the thought of the night ahead was never far from her mind. She slipped her arm through Luke's, murmuring for his ears only. "I think we're about done here, don't you?"

He surveyed the crowd before turning back to her. "They're about to announce the results of the auction. Let's stay for that and then we can go."

"But we didn't bid on anything."

"You didn't, but I did while you were chatting to your client."

"So what did you bid on?"

"I'll tell you if I win," he replied smugly, patting the hand that was holding the crook of his arm. A drink waiter with laden tray wandered past, and after extricating himself from Angela's clutch, Luke took two champagne flutes from the tray and handed one to Angela. "I think I need a drink."

It *was* getting warmer in the venue. Perhaps he should be drinking water instead. Her thoughts were interrupted by the amplified voice of the emcee.

"Ladies and gentlemen—if you direct your eyes and ears this way, I'm almost ready to read out the results of the auction. Before I do, I should remind you of the importance of this fund-raising event. Through your generosity tonight, some talented young swimmers will have the opportunity to travel and compete on the world stage." He paused before the expectant crowd. "If anyone would like to increase their bid to secure the item of their dreams, now is the time. I will give you five more minutes before the bidding papers are removed and brought to me."

Guests hurried back to the display tables, checking the status of their bid and debating whether they needed to increase their offer.

Angela looked to Luke, who hadn't moved. "Aren't you going to check your bid?"

"Nope. I think I made it high enough to win that one. I'm working on the theory that anyone who has the capacity to bid more than me wouldn't need what's on offer."

"I like a man who's sure of himself," she said dryly. "Does this confidence spill over into other areas of your life as well?"

"Mostly. You've seen that for yourself. The secret is to never let on when you aren't confident." He looked back to the podium. "I think the bidding really is finished now." He gave her a wink and took a sip of his wine. "We'll see how my stance has paid off."

She shook her head in bemusement. Lord knows what he was buying. Probably a bottle of vintage Grange Hermitage. It was a drop keenly sought by collectors and she had already seen he had an impressive wine collection. The paintings weren't his thing, and surely he wasn't buying any of the jewellery items.

As the emcee ran through his patter about each item, images were displayed on the screen behind them. Some people scored a bargain and others had paid top dollar as a result of their bid. It was all for a good cause. The wine appeared on the screen, but the name of the successful bidder wasn't Luke. Angela looked at him to gauge his reaction, but he didn't seem at all perturbed. There wasn't much left, only…

"And finally, ladies and gentlemen, we have the major offer of the evening. The Lady Juno is available for a fortnight, fully staffed and ready to go. Just bring your personal effects. And the winning bidder is… Luke Johnson."

There was polite clapping and a man nearby clapped Luke on the shoulder. "Well done, mate. That would be fabulous trip but I couldn't top your offer."

"You bought it!" Angela was incredulous.

"No, I didn't buy the yacht; I just paid for the opportunity to take the cruise on offer."

"I'm amazed. What prompted you to bid for that?"

"Don't you think it would provide a wonderful opportunity for a honeymoon?"

What did he say?

It was not often she was lost for words. She stared at him, unsure of what was happening. There was noise surrounding them, but none of it penetrated her bubble of consciousness as she stared up at him.

"Angela, I didn't plan this in advance so I don't have a ring right now. I am absolutely not going to drop on one knee in front of this crowd, but will you marry me?"

"You want to marry me?"

"Isn't that what I just said? You might like a say in choosing the ring, so we could do that together."

"But why?"

"Why what? Why choose the ring? I know you're particular about that sort of thing."

"Of course that's not what I mean. Why do you want to marry me?"

"I would have thought that was obvious. Because I love you. Because I want to share my life with you. Because I think what we have together is damn special."

Tears threatened to overflow. She had thought she would never hear him say those words. Her heart was about to explode. The choking sensation in her throat made it difficult to breathe.

"Angela? Are you saying the answer's no? Have I totally misunderstood your feelings for me?"

"No, you stupid man. Of course I love you. I have for so long."

"So it's yes?"

She moved closer, grasping his forearms and looking earnestly up at him. "You understand that Mattie and I are a package deal. Marriage to me is not a simple affair."

"You mean I get two for the price of one?" Luke released her grip on his arms and with one finger tilted her chin upwards. He dropped a light kiss on her lips. "Listen to me. Hear me, woman. I want to marry you and want to welcome your son into my life as well. He's a great kid. Both of you will make me a very happy man." The intensity of the look he gave her would have melted icebergs at twenty paces.

254

"Say you're happy. Say you'll marry me and we can sail off into the sunset."

She stared at him, blinking her emotions under control. She loved this man so much. When she spoke, her voice was strained and husky. "I thought you'd never ask. Of course I'll marry you."

He pulled her towards him in passionate embrace. The hunger with which he claimed her lips was reflected in the slow burn in the pit of her belly and radiating outwards. She could feel the evidence of his arousal. *Not here*! Pulling back, she could see a slow flush infuse his face and repressed the urge to giggle.

A voice broke into their private reverie. "Hey Luke— save the hot stuff for later, mate. You're required over at the auction table. A small matter of payment, I believe. Congratulations. That sounds like the trip of a lifetime."

It would be. More than the man realised. Angela moved to stand in front of Luke, aware he was taking a deep breath and attempting to quell his obvious ardour.

"Thank you, Edward. I'll be there in a minute." Luke turned back to Angela with a wicked smile. "Hold those thoughts. I'll sign their paperwork and then we'll clear out of here."

She swept back a lock of hair from her eyes, noting the promise in his. "There's no hurry. We've all the time in the world."

He winked at her in response, before pushing his way through the crowd. She watched his progress to the auction table, interrupted by a couple of back-slapping well-wishers who had no idea what the congratulations should really be for. They had a shared future; Luke, Mattie and her. That was so unbelievably fabulous. From here on, it would be Thursday every day of the week.

Maria cooked a fabulous meal on the last evening in which Angela, Louise and Mattie stayed at Luke's home. She served them Chicken Cacciatore, Braised Broccolini, and Roasted Rosemary Potatoes.
If you would like to receive a copy of the recipe for these dishes, you can do so via this link. https://sendfox.com/lp/1rxkxz

If you enjoyed this story, you may like to read **Ambition and Passion.** Available at your favourite eBook retailer.

No excuses, no regrets. Miranda almost believed it too. As her business grew, her love life bombed. Had luck deserted her when she needed it most?
books2read.com/Ambition-and-Passion

Before you go...

You finished the book – great news.

I'd love to hear your thoughts after reading *Maison Angelique*. There are several ways you can do that:
- emailing me at emily@emilyhussey.com.au
- posting on Facebook at https://www.facebook.com/EmilyHusseyAuthor/
- posting on Goodreads at https://www.goodreads.com/Emily_Hussey
- leaving a review online at place of purchase.

Your comments will help me in providing more great stories and will interest future readers.

Emily Hussey

Rowena Wylde

Rowena writes in a seaside suburb
in metropolitan Adelaide, South
Australia. She loves writing stories
that are character focused, but the
plot-line keeps the reader
entertained as well. Her characters
sometime surprise her with the
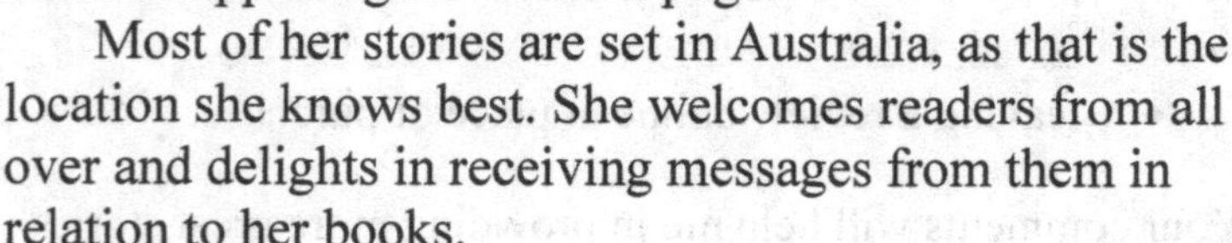
things they say and do – it's always interesting to see
what's happening on the next page.

Most of her stories are set in Australia, as that is the
location she knows best. She welcomes readers from all
over and delights in receiving messages from them in
relation to her books.

https://linktr.ee/rowenawylde
Email: rowenawylde@gmail.com

Emily Hussey

Having lived in several Australian states, Emily Hussey now lives in a coastal suburb of Adelaide in South Australia. She spent her twenties in Alice Springs, which became the setting for the Red Centre Series.

Emily enjoys the short story format, and has been published in local anthologies. The genres range from crime to romance, with some contemporary fiction for good measure.

She was a marriage celebrant for 24 years, and has married couples in different locations, ranging from private gardens, to beaches, to caves or rural locations. Many of her clients remain friends to this day.

She usually writes with a black cat at her elbow, demanding an equal share of attention. Writing tends to be fuelled with regular coffee boosts, and occasional squares of very dark chocolate.

Website: http://emilyhussey.com.au,
Email: emily@emilyhussey.com.au

Ambition and Passion

When Miranda Montgomery convinced Hugh Paterson to award her company the hospital contract, she didn't envision the sacrifice it would entail. Her company's survival depends upon it. A pity he's such a misogynist jerk. She can give as good as she gets, but has to play the game if she's going to keep him onside.

Working in close proximity was unavoidable, and Miranda was surprised to discover the creative side of his personality. Not quite as surprised as discovering the hot body and passion beneath that business suit. It was a lust equally matched by hers.

The attraction between them sizzles, but office romances are bad news. It's already apparent others would sabotage her business if they could, and Miranda must use her wits to survive.

For the sake of her employees, she has to put the contract first. After all – she and Hugh can pick up where they left off when the contract is finished. At least, that's what she thought. She never expected Hugh to leave her alone at Christmas.

books2read.com/Ambition-and-Passion